MW01487382

SECRET

OBSESSION

RED STONE SECURITY SERIES

Katie Reus

Cover art: Jaycee of Sweet 'N Spicy Designs
Editor: Julia Ganis, JuliaEdits.com
Author website: http://www.katiereus.com

Secret Obsession/Katie Reus. -- 1st ed.

ISBN-10: 1942447485
ISBN-13: 9781942447481

eISBN: 9781942447474

For my husband, who puts his life on the line for strangers every day.

Praise for the novels of Katie Reus

"Sexy military romantic suspense!" —USA Today

"…a wild hot ride for readers. The story grabs you and doesn't let go."
—*New York Times* bestselling author, Cynthia Eden

"Has all the right ingredients: a hot couple, evil villains, and a killer
action-filled plot. . . . [The] Moon Shifter series is what I call Grade-
A entertainment!" —Joyfully Reviewed

"I could not put this book down. . . . Let me be clear that I am not
saying that this was a good book *for* a paranormal genre; it was an
excellent romance read, *period.*" —All About Romance

"Reus strikes just the right balance of steamy sexual tension and nail-
biting action….This romantic thriller reliably hits every note that
fans of the genre will expect." —*Publishers Weekly*

"Prepare yourself for the start of a great new series! . . . I'm excited
about reading more about this great group of characters."
—Fresh Fiction

"Wow! This powerful, passionate hero sizzles with sheer
deliciousness. I loved every sexy twist of this fun & exhilarating tale.
Katie Reus delivers!" —Carolyn Crane, RITA award winning author

Continued…

CHAPTER ONE

Raegan was practically vibrating with energy as she shut down her computer. She couldn't remember the last Friday she'd actually gotten to leave at five o'clock. She loved her new job at Red Stone Security, but working with Athena in the new marketing/PR division kept them incredibly busy. Late nights and weekends were standard—the benefits and money were freaking worth the crazy hours. And she took full advantage when she was off, enjoying everything Miami had to offer.

"What are your plans for tonight?" Athena asked, stepping out of her office, a big smile on her face.

Raegan knew exactly why she was so happy too. She got to go home to her sexy fiancé. Even though Athena was only two years older than her, she seemed to have her shit together in a way Raegan could admit she envied a teeny bit. She'd traveled the world as an event planner for two years after getting a job at Red Stone and was so put together.

Raegan felt like an imposter most of the time. She'd grown up on a farm, hadn't seen much of the world, and she knew people thought she'd gotten this job because she was Keith Caldwell's niece. Which was sorta true. Of course, she wouldn't have kept her job if she wasn't good at it. "Going dancing with your cousin-in-law-to-be. Or whatever Dominique will be to you soon."

"Let me guess, Ruby and Julieta are going too?"

Raegan snorted as she pulled out the small gift bag she'd tucked into her desk drawer, and stood. "Yes, which means Ivan will be there as a brooding bodyguard." It was actually nice that Ivan went out with them. He was such a huge, scary-looking guy he kept pretty much all jerks away from them.

Raegan loved dancing but that didn't mean she wanted to grind with every guy on the dance floor, and it seemed most guys couldn't take a hint. It was like they thought that simply because she was dancing with her friends she needed a dance partner, and then said dance partner got to rub all over her. No thank you.

"Good. Remember the buddy system," Athena said, falling in step with her as they headed toward the elevators. "And watch your drink at all times. And—"

"Oh my God, I'm going to start calling you Mom if you don't stop." Raegan pressed both the up and down buttons on the elevator keypad. "I'm going to see Porter," she said when Athena raised an eyebrow.

"Okay, well, I'm allowed to worry. I can't help it. You're the best assistant I've ever had and I don't like change, so if something happened to you I'd have to train someone else," she grumbled.

"You're such a liar." Raegan knew Athena felt guilty over the kidnapping. She'd been extra protective since Vegas. As if she could have prevented what happened. Raegan had simply been in the wrong place at the wrong time when Athena had been targeted by a nut job and had gotten kidnapped along with her.

Athena just shrugged. "Oh, Harrison wanted to know if we could both attend the Celebration of Chefs event tomorrow night. I know it's last minute so I told him yes for me but maybe for you. Absolutely no pressure. This is just something fun for us but he wanted us—"

"I'm actually going already."

Athena raised an eyebrow as her elevator arrived. She held her hand in between the doors so they wouldn't close on her, but didn't get in. "As in, with a date?"

"No, just as friends."

Now her boss and friend's eyes narrowed. "Is this with a certain billionaire who your cousins hate?"

Raegan resisted the urge to roll her eyes. "They don't hate him and I'm not having this conversation again. Just tell Harrison I'll be there." When her elevator dinged she ducked into it and called out, "Have fun with your sexy man tonight!"

Athena grumbled something but Raegan missed most of it as the elevator door whooshed closed. She adored her older cousins but they were ridiculously overprotective. Because of their age differences and because she'd never left the Midwest until almost a year ago, she'd never been close to them. But now that she lived in Miami and worked for their company it was like she had three older brothers who thought every man was an enemy. And they'd apparently recruited Athena into their way of thinking.

Raegan might not have much world experience, but she'd been fending off the opposite sex since she was fourteen. She could take care of herself.

Besides, there was only one man she was interested in and he seemed to have absolutely zero attraction to her. She'd never even seen a flicker of awareness from him, which, perversely, made her want the sexy cop even more.

So there was no reason she shouldn't do whatever she wanted with whoever she wanted. But she hadn't been lying to Athena—tomorrow she was just going to the Celebrity Chef event with a friend.

The soft elevator music flowed into another bland song as the car arrived on the floor for one of her adorable, overprotective cousins: Porter Caldwell.

When she reached the plush office of his assistant, she was surprised to find it empty. The door to Porter's office was cracked open and she heard male voices. Normally she wouldn't interrupt, but she heard both Porter and Grant talking and knew they wouldn't mind.

After a light knock she started to step into the office, but felt all the air rush out of her lungs when she saw that it wasn't just Porter and Grant, but Ford Burke as well.

The sexy man made her feel like that naïve little farm girl she'd been trying to shed. Just looking at him turned her knees to mush. He was tall, with ridiculously broad shoulders she wanted to run her fingers over. He kept his dark hair closely cropped and had a neatly trimmed beard that on most guys she wouldn't have liked. She'd never been a fan of facial hair until Ford. But she'd had a fantasy or two of what it would feel like to have his face buried between her—

She blinked when she realized they were all staring at her. She felt her cheeks heat up and wanted to kick her own butt. Raegan wasn't sure if they'd said anything to her directly so, holding up the little gift bag, she said, "I brought this for Maddox."

Just like that, Porter's normally hard expression softened. "You spoil him," he murmured, moving away from the desk, a grin on his face.

"Of course I do. I'm going to hold onto the title of favorite older cousin forever and I have no shame buying his love." During her lunch break today she'd found a cute little boutique downtown and snagged an adorable Darth Vader pajama set. On the front of the shirt it said 'Not Afraid of the Dark Side.'

Laughing, Porter kissed her forehead and pulled her into a light embrace. "You coming by for dinner tonight?"

"I can't. Plans with the girls. It's why I wanted to bring this to you now. But I'll stop by tomorrow to see my little man." She didn't want kids of her own for years yet, but little Maddox had completely stolen her heart. He'd just turned one last month and was walking and babbling like a little maniac. And she loved spoiling him.

She was vaguely aware of Ford watching her, but of course he was—she'd interrupted them. She wished his focus was on her for other reasons.

"Where are you guys going tonight?" Grant asked and before she turned to face him she could hear the frown in his voice.

"None of your business," she said cheekily, giving him a frown of her own when she saw the plethora of weapons on Porter's desk. "What the heck is this? Are you guys starting your own army?"

To her surprise, Grant's cheeks flushed the faintest shade of pink. "Maybe don't say anything to Belle about this?"

Now that surprised Raegan. As far as she knew her cousins didn't keep anything from their wives. "Um, about what? Your new arsenal?" She eyed the guns again. They all looked really old.

He nodded at Ford. "They're antiques and Ford's helping me refurbish them."

Raegan smiled at Ford, murmured "Hi," and he just nodded, his expression the same as it always was. Brooding.

Grant just continued. "Once they're in good shape they'll be worth a lot but…"

"Belle gets annoyed with too many guns around the house?" Raegan guessed. She'd grown up on a farm so she was no stranger to guns, especially not rifles, but she'd seen how some of the guys at Red Stone acted around their guns. They might as well stroke them and start calling them 'my precious.'

"Well, we're…pregnant and—"

"Belle's pregnant?"

"Yeah and she's really emotional right now and wanted me to get rid of all my guns so I'm waiting to tell her about this…" He trailed off, shrugging.

Raegan pulled him into a big hug. "Congrats! How far along is she?" she asked, stepping back.

"About four months. We wanted to wait until she was a little past the first trimester, but we were going to announce it next week."

"That's great. I'm so happy for you guys."

"Thanks." He grinned in a way she'd never seen. A mix of pride and a little bit of terror. Which was just way too adorable.

She heard her phone buzz in her purse, knew it would be Dominique telling her to hurry up. A relief, since it would get her out of here and away from Ford's penetrating gaze. "I've gotta run, but can I call Belle and congratulate her?"

"Yeah, of course. Why don't you come over for dinner Sunday? Her mom gave us a couple casseroles," he tacked on when she would have automatically asked if he was cooking or Belle was.

"I'll be there." After giving her two cousins another quick hug, she nodded once at Ford, who'd been quiet as usual. "Nice to see you again, Ford."

He just watched her with that brooding stare he seemed to have down pat, and made a sort of grunting sound that could have meant any number of things. And damn it, she kinda liked it. Which was ridiculous. She was no one to him. Just Grant, Porter and Harrison's younger cousin.

Just as she reached the door, Porter said, "Hey, are you going to the Celebration of Chefs event tomorrow night? Harrison said something about you and Athena maybe going. If you are, you can catch a ride with me and Lizzy."

Thanks to Porter's generosity she was renting a one-bedroom condo in the same high rise he lived in with his wife. Many, many floors below them, and her place was a lot smaller, but it was a great home. She knew they'd bought it as an investment and had been planning to rent it out, and when they'd offered to let her rent it, it had been impossible to say no. Partially because of the way they'd guilt-tripped her into it but also because it was a safe place and they'd given her such a great deal.

"I won't need a ride, but thanks. I'm going with someone." When her phone started ringing she used it as an excuse to race out of there before they could question her about her 'date' that wasn't actually a date. They wouldn't see it that way though.

She actually had gone on one date with him back in Vegas but since then she'd made it clear she just wanted to be friends and he was okay with it.

She'd dated other guys in Miami since, but nothing ever went past the first date. And she knew it was because she was so incredibly attracted to Ford "too sexy for his own good" Burke.

* * *

"What's that look?" Ford asked as Grant and Porter exchanged an annoyed glance between them. Now that Raegan was out of the room he could finally breathe again. The woman made him crazy. She was a combination of sweetness and jaw-dropping sexiness. Impossible to resist.

"Nothing," Grant muttered, turning back to the desk. But he looked at his brother again. "You see the way she ran out of here?"

Porter went back to his standard stoic mode now that Raegan was gone, and nodded once. "I bet she's going out with that dick again and didn't want to tell us."

Ford didn't like the sound of that. At all. Sweet Raegan had had him twisted up for damn near eleven months. He'd met her at a few of the Caldwell family functions and each time it was like he forgot to act like a human. He couldn't even talk to her, and he'd never been nervous around women. Hell, he'd done undercover work for a year back when he'd been on the drug task force. He was comfortable around people as a rule.

But around Raegan? He was a moron.

She was a decade younger than him, or at least close to it. He didn't think she was older than twenty-three. And that made him feel ancient and a little bit like a perv. But he couldn't help it.

She had that girl-next-door thing going on and it pushed all his buttons. If she'd been anyone but Grant and Porter's cousin he'd have asked her out by now. Or at least tried to. Because God knew talking didn't come easy when she was around.

He cleared his throat. "What dick?"

Grant crossed his arms over his chest as he leaned against the front of the desk, looking every bit the intimidating detective he'd once been. He'd nearly died in an explosion almost two years ago, and half his face and upper body had been burned, scarred because of it. Right now he looked ready to take someone's head off. "Some British guy she met in Vegas. They're just friends, supposedly, but...why would a guy keep taking her out when he's in town if they're just friends?"

"Especially one like that," Porter muttered, starting to put one of the rifles back into its case.

"Like what?" He'd never asked about Raegan, had basically forced himself not to ask Grant about her, but screw that if this British guy was bad news.

"Some rich prick," Grant practically snarled.

"Harrison said he was inquiring about using our services," Porter tacked on, using a terrible British accent.

It was like the two men had devolved to adolescents, but he understood the sentiment. Raegan was beautiful, no doubt, but she was sweet and way too kind for her own good from what he'd seen. The kind of woman assholes would like to prey on.

Ford rubbed the back of his neck, forcing himself not to ask any more questions. No good would come of it. He didn't need to know who she was or wasn't dating. Even if he hadn't been able to fuck anyone else since meeting her. His dick knew what it wanted: Raegan. He had good taste, that was for sure.

When she'd walked into Porter's office wearing that slim pencil skirt, pretty pink top and high heels, all his naughty librarian fantasies had flared to life. She was lean, with a runner's build, and had long, thick dark hair he'd fantasized about running his hands through as he claimed her mouth.

Then her body.

He always had the urge to mess up her perfect hair, to get a rise out of her just to see her cheeks flush pink. And he always froze like a teenager around her.

As the two brothers continued to talk about the merits of Raegan's date and how they'd like to kick his ass, Ford started packing up the rest of the rifles. Grant had found them at a yard sale, of all places, and snatched them up for a steal. Now he wanted Ford's help to restore them. Some wouldn't be worth much more than the money they put into refurbishing them, but a couple Grant would be able to sell to collectors if he didn't keep them himself. It was a solid investment.

"...and BDSM. What the hell?"

Ford snapped back to reality at the last few words snarled by Grant. "BDSM?" They couldn't still be talking about Raegan. Could they?

Grant slid the last rusted rifle into the long, padded case. His expression was disgusted. "I ran the guy Raegan's 'not dating' and yeah, turns out he's into that shit. Owns a couple clubs. But she's a grown woman. We can't tell her what to do."

"She's really not dating him. At least that's what Lizzy says." Porter lifted a shoulder but Ford could see the tension humming in the man's body.

Ford gritted his teeth and turned away from them, making himself look busy. He wanted to ask what the guy's name was, do a run on the guy himself. Only that was insane behavior. He rolled his shoulders once. He had no claim on Raegan. She barely looked at him.

"You guys mind if I head out? I promised a buddy I'd do some light recon tonight. We're trying to track down some guy they suspect of a bunch of jewelry store burglaries." At some downtown club that wasn't remotely his style, but it was overtime and he owed the detective a favor.

"I'll walk down with you," Grant said. "You want to take these now?"

He nodded, picking up two of the cases. Anything to get his mind off Raegan and why he could never have her.

CHAPTER TWO

He kept his hood pulled up over his head as he watched Raegan on the dance floor of the loud, obnoxious club. In a place like this the hood didn't stand out and it kept his face blocked from any security cameras. He'd seen enough guys wearing hoodies, sunglasses and ridiculous bling that he wasn't even a blip on anyone's radar tonight. Just another club-goer.

He wasn't even sure if he'd make a move tonight, but he liked to think two steps ahead of everyone. So if an opportunity presented itself, he'd take it.

It was how he'd come to be where he was.

She was such a fucking tease. It would be easy to write her off as another Miami whore, but he knew she wasn't like that. But she constantly teased him, made him crazy. She was so nice to him, always smiling at him, asking him how his day was, what his weekend plans were. He wondered if she knew what she was doing, if that big-eyed farm-girl thing was all an act designed to make him sweat.

Right now she sure as hell didn't appear as if she'd stepped off any farm. The dance floor was outside and looked out over the white sand beach. Strings of colored lights were the only roof for everyone out there.

But he stayed back at the main bar, his seat giving him the perfect view of her and her friends. Unfortunately she'd come with three other girls and three men. He'd seen them before too. Well, all except one of the men. A guy with a messed-up face who looked like he might be related to the other Hispanic man.

The big blond guy with them looked like a damn Viking and he rarely left the table where the women's drinks were. The guy with the ugly face didn't leave often either, but he was watching one of the blonde women who was friends with Raegan on the dance floor. He never seemed to take his eyes off the curvy woman.

Raegan was a lot leaner than her friends. Slim, but with enough curves that she was smoking hot. As the music shifted to a slower, more sensual song, he watched as the Hispanic guy at the table stood, moved closer to the dance floor. As if he couldn't keep away from the blonde.

The Viking stayed at the table, unfortunately. Still...he might be able to make this work. If he could get her loose, pliant, he could get her the hell out of here. Then she'd be his to do what he wanted with. He tossed a bill on the bar and stood, drink in hand. As soon as he'd taken three steps his seat was already occupied, no surprise.

The Latin beat of the music vibrated through him, pumped up his adrenaline as he reached into the pocket of his pants. Just having the small container was a schedule-one felony but it was easily disposable. He was going to use it now anyway.

Always be prepared. His motto.

Tonight he'd just planned to follow Raegan like usual, but given this opportunity, he had to take advantage. He was always ready for an opening because he knew one day, he'd get one. Normally she was surrounded by people, even at work. And her condo building was difficult to get into. Not impossible, but they had more security than a place like this did.

It would be easier to lead her away once he got this drug in her system. He'd have to break her away from her pack of friends. That would be the difficult part. Getting her dosed was also difficult, but he was up for the challenge. And if he failed, no harm, no foul. She'd never know he'd done a damn thing. That was the most important part. She couldn't know he'd been here, what he'd done.

He was going to spend time with Raegan alone. Naked. With no other distractions. Then she'd see how good they could be together. She was always so nice to him, but...she didn't seem to see the real him. That was all he wanted. He wanted her to see him, to touch him, to tell him how much she wanted him.

Winding his way through the throng of half-dressed people, he felt secure enough that he blended in with everyone else. Standing out was the one thing he couldn't do.

As he passed the table where the blond giant was sitting, watching the cadre of women he'd come with, he didn't bother trying to move up behind him out of his line of sight. Instead, he acted as if he'd go around him, then tripped, spilling his drink on the guy's pants.

He grabbed onto the man's shoulder as he weaved on his feet. "Shit, man, I'm sorry." He intentionally slurred, using sleight of hand to dump the liquid into Raegan's glass on the table.

The guy shrugged off his hold, his expression hard as he stared at him. "It's fine. Move along."

"Yeah, yeah, really sorry." Keeping his head low, he held up his hands as he hurried off, blending into the crowd of people and high top tables behind him. He didn't turn around even though he wanted to. He wouldn't look to see if the Viking had noticed what he'd done. Maybe the guy would remember his face, maybe not. It wouldn't matter. No one could pin anything on him anyway.

Adrenaline humming through him, he kept his pace steady. He needed to find another spot so he could watch Raegan unobtrusively. If his move had worked, he'd get Raegan alone a lot sooner than he'd planned.

And then he'd do all the things he'd been fantasizing about.

* * *

Raegan pressed a hand to her stomach as a wave of nausea swept through her. Blinking, she shook herself. She'd only had two drinks, but it had started to get hot. Even with the huge fans and chilly breeze kicking up from the Atlantic it was getting sticky. Summer in Miami wasn't remotely cold anyway, but the place kept huge misting fans blowing to cool everyone off. That wasn't working right now.

She'd worn a brightly colored halter wraparound dress but that didn't seem to matter now. She needed fresher air, ASAP. There was a live DJ tonight and he'd been playing mostly Latin dance. The beat of the music seemed suddenly too loud, pounding in her head, every-thing too stifling. There were too many people. She felt suffocated.

She started to tell Ruby she needed some water, but she noticed that Montez had finally worked up the courage to do more than just stare at the blonde bombshell. They weren't exactly dancing, but they were talking near the dance floor. That was progress. Sandro and Dominique were still tearing it up. Though Sandro didn't have a chance with Dominique, that much Raegan knew. And Julieta and Ivan might be at the same table as her, but they were in their own world.

She started to tell them that she was going to grab a bottle of water, but slid off her chair instead when Ivan leaned down to his fiancée's ear and started whispering something that made Julieta laugh and blush.

"I'm gonna grab a water," she murmured, not sure if they'd heard her, and at this point she didn't really care.

The huge bar was half inside and half outside the building. But she knew there was also a small tiki bar on the other side of the expansive dance floor overlooking the beach and ocean.

It seemed to take forever to get to the edge of the dance floor where larger seating like couches and plush lounge chairs were set up. She knew this place was popular for beachgoers and transitioned to more of a club at night. According to Julieta it was one of the top-rated clubs in Miami because of the fun atmosphere and celebrity sightings.

Not that Raegan had seen anyone famous. Or she didn't think she had. And right now, she didn't care. She just needed water and a cool blast of air.

As she continued on through a throng of people, another wave of nausea combined with dizziness assaulted her.

She blinked, clutching on to a high top table. The occupants, three college-age-looking guys grinned at her.

"Buy you a drink?" one of them asked.

She couldn't even shake her head, couldn't say much of anything. Instead she dropped her hand and continued walking. Her body felt numb, and the floor was beginning to tilt, but she knew she didn't want to sit there with a bunch of frat boys.

Something was wrong with her, she wasn't sure what, but it was getting worse and she was getting worried. Instead of continuing toward the tiki bar she turned back around.

She needed to find her friends. And go home.

"You okay?" A man wearing a hoodie and jeans sidled up to her, put his arm around her waist to steady her.

She tried to answer but struggled to find her voice. The scent of his cologne turned her stomach even more. She shook her head. Or tried to.

"Let's get you some fresh air," he said, guiding her back through the thick mass of people.

The bright lights above suddenly seemed like a manic kaleidoscope of colors, flashing and hurting her eyes. She was barely aware of moving, but when he shoved open a big door that opened up onto a short set of stairs that led to the sandy beach, she tried to pull back.

She didn't want to go to the beach or anywhere with this stranger. "Leave me alone," she said. Or tried to. Her words came out slurred.

His grip on her upper arm tightened as he shoved her through the door.

She cried out and tried to turn back around but he slammed the door shut.

Iciness invaded her veins as she tripped and fell into the sand. This was not good. She needed to call her friends. Get help. Waves crashed in the distance and she could hear the thrum of laughter, voices and music through the big wall behind her, but she knew that no one could help her now. Even if she screamed. And she couldn't find her voice. Everything was all screwed up. God, what was wrong with her?

Before she could push up, strong arms yanked her to her feet.

"Don't know why you're wearing these stupid heels," the guy muttered, tugging her close. As if he had a right to touch her at all. He wrapped an arm around her waist but she shoved at him.

Or, again, tried. Panic punched through her, but her fingers wouldn't obey as he dragged her across the sand. She lost one of her shoes in her struggle. "Let...me go." Her words didn't come out as strong as she'd intended.

"Hey!" A deep, vaguely familiar male voice from behind seemed as if it was coming from a long way away. "What the fuck are you doing?" He was angry.

"No, no, no," the guy holding her muttered.

Suddenly she was falling, her knees and hands hitting the soft sand. The grains rolled across her knees and palms. She tried to push up, but another wave of dizziness swelled through her.

She was aware of someone calling her name. Someone...familiar. She couldn't place the voice, could barely remember her own name, as callused, strong hands gripped her upper arms and pulled her to her feet.

CHAPTER THREE

F ord pulled Raegan to her feet as gently as he could. "Are you okay, sweetheart?" The term of endearment just slipped out, but she didn't seem to notice.

She blinked at him with big, blue eyes. "Ford?"

He held onto her upper arms. "Did you know that guy?" Right about now he wanted to race after the asshole who'd shoved her and run, but no way was he leaving Raegan to fend for herself. Not when she could barely stand.

"What guy?" She blinked again, swaying in his arms now.

Cursing, he glanced over his shoulder as the side door to the beach club opened. A giggling group of three women stumbled out. Instead of heading their way, they turned and started for what he knew was the parking lot. He turned back to Raegan, who was beginning to fade fast.

He cupped her cheek, shook her a little. Her eyes were glazed. "How much have you had to drink?"

"What...you doing here?"

Damn it, she was drunk. Or...worse. "Who did you come with?" Because it sure as hell hadn't been that guy.

Instead of answering, she wrapped her arms around him, pressing her very full breasts against his chest as she

practically nuzzled his neck. "You smell good," she murmured.

He groaned at the feel of her pressed up against him,
felt like a dick for liking it so much. "Listen, sweetheart,
we need to get you out of here." Without pause, he lifted
her into his arms, holding her close. She had one of those
slim wallet-sized purses with the strap securely around
her wrist. He scooped up her fallen shoe as they passed it,
tried not to notice the soft swell of her breasts peeking
out of her halter dress as she cuddled against him. Or the
way she was rubbing his chest and nuzzling his neck.

"Who did you come with, Raegan?" he asked as he carried her along the exterior of the club. It was just chance
he'd seen her stumbling out the side door with some
shady-looking guy. He'd come here tonight because a detective friend had needed a favor. A suspect they were trying to bring in was known to frequent this place and half
a dozen others. This was the club he'd been chosen to
stake out.

"Friends. Who'd you come with? Your...girlfriend?"
Her words were still slurred, uneven.

"Don't have one," he muttered. Because the only
woman he wanted was currently in his arms. And she
wouldn't be acting like this if she were sober. That much
he knew.

The music faded as he made his way past the door
they'd come out of. As he rounded the building, he noticed two security guys talking and smoking. They didn't
even give him a second glance as he carried a practically
unconscious woman into the parking lot. Not doing their

damn job. He knew who the owner of this place was and he'd be making a call to him very soon.

But Raegan was his priority. When they reached his truck, he got her into the passenger-side seat.

"You smell good," she said again, this time nipping his earlobe. Her voice was sensual, her eyes heavy-lidded as she looked at him.

Inches separated them as he stared into blue, blue eyes. Eyes he could drown in. Looking at her now, however, he wondered if she'd been drugged. "So do you," he said quietly. "I need you to focus for a second. I'm going to take you to see a friend of mine." Because Ford was pretty sure she'd been drugged, and that guy who'd ditched her had clearly had something bad planned. "He's a doctor—"

She listed forward suddenly but when he went to steady her, she grabbed onto his shirt and tugged him down to her. Her mouth skated over his, her lips soft and pliable.

He needed to pull back. To stop this. Right now. She wasn't herself, wasn't thinking.

But when she moaned against him and bit his bottom lip, he lost the ability to think. Almost.

"Raegan, no." He withdrew from her, strapped her in, slid back and shut the door as she made a protesting sound.

Cursing, he leaned against the side of the door, scrubbed a hand over his face. Raegan was not for him and she wouldn't even remember the kiss anyway. He shouldn't have let it go that far. Continuing to curse himself, he rounded the truck and slid into the front seat.

"Do you remember how much you had to drink?" he asked, starting the ignition.

"Um...two. Maybe one and a half. I started to feel...dizzy though. Why are you here again?" She closed her eyes, let her head fall back.

Damn it. Drugs. He decided then and there that he would make it his personal mission to find out who the hell had drugged her. Because this clearly wasn't a case of her drinking too much. "Open your eyes," he said sharply, rolling down her window to get a burst of air rolling over her.

Her phone started to ring in her purse and he guessed it might be one of her friends wondering where she was. "You want to check who that is?"

"Um...hold on." It took her a few tries to get her small purse unzipped and when she did she squinted at the screen. "It's Jules."

"Is that who you came with?"

"Yesh," she slurred out, her eyes starting to droop again.

He plucked it from her hand, not bothering to ask for permission as he swiped his thumb across the screen. "This is Ford Burke. I'm with the Miami PD and I'm taking Raegan to a doctor."

"Oh my God! Is she okay?" the woman named Jules shouted. He could hear music and other voices in the background.

"She's fine." Or she would be. He wouldn't let anything happen to her.

"What's going on, then? Why are you taking her to a doctor?" Her voice was bordering on panic.

"I found some guy trying to take her out of the club and realized it's likely she's been drugged. I'm friends with her cousins, Grant, Porter and Harrison. I used to work with Grant. Please call him and confirm."

"What hospital are you taking her to? We'll meet you there."

"Not taking her to a hospital." Because the ER on a Friday night was a nightmare. Didn't matter that he was a cop. That would only get him so far in the favor department. She'd still have to wait hours to be looked at. They'd check her vitals, stick her in a room with three other people and come back and check on her when they could—and that was only after they finally got her to a damn room. No way was he going to put her through that when he could get her looked at immediately.

"I'm taking her to a local clinic. Friend of mine runs it. Call Grant and confirm who I am. You know his number?"

"Uh, yeah. Well, my fiancé does. He's with me. He works with Grant."

"Good. She's fine. I've got her phone and she doesn't need to deal with a bunch of people down at the clinic."

"I don't know how this happened. We were all together, then when I turned around she was just gone. I thought maybe she'd gone to the bathroom or to grab another drink, but then none of us could find her. Is she really okay?"

"Yeah. I think...someone slipped her Rohypnol." He didn't want her friend to freak out even more, but decided to be honest. It was also known as a date rape drug, something he guessed her friend knew by her worried gasp.

"There's no way!"

He turned on his blinker as he neared the turnoff to his friend's clinic. The neighborhood bordered a sketchy area of town, but that was sorta the point of the clinic's location. People who needed medical care the most often couldn't get it. His friend tried to combat that problem by providing affordable medical care. In some cases, free. And he was better equipped to give Raegan his complete attention as opposed to the harried, Friday night ER staff at a hospital. If Ford had been worried she'd overdosed he'd have taken her straight there.

"Well it happened. Look, I gotta go. Gotta get her inside now. Call Grant, confirm to make yourself feel better. I'm sure she'll call you in the morning. She's safe, I swear." He cut her off before she could respond. He didn't care if it was rude. Being polite wasn't a concern right now. Raegan was his only concern.

"I've never heard you talk so much at once." Raegan giggled a little as she watched him.

He was glad she was awake, but having all her focus on him was jarring. "How're you feeling?"

"Funny. You think I was drugged?" She giggled again, softer this time.

"Maybe."

"I've never done drugs. And I'm not saying that because you're a cop. A very sexy cop." She laughed at that, seeming to think it was hilarious.

"We're going inside here," he said, nodding at the darkened clinic. It was late but he knew his friend was still here in the back. He always stayed until midnight even though he locked the doors—to keep out would-be thieves and junkies looking for a fix.

"You sure it's open?"

"Yeah." He was out and to her side in seconds. He hated that someone had done this to her, but he'd worry about finding the guilty party later. Right now he just needed to make sure she was safe.

* * *

Montez frowned, listening to Ivan talking to Grant Caldwell on the phone. They'd all left the club after his sister Julieta had talked to some guy on Raegan's phone. Some guy who claimed he was a cop and was allegedly taking her to a clinic.

Now they were in the parking lot, waiting while Ivan talked to Grant, confirming whether this was true. He hated the thought of anything happening to Raegan. Hell, any woman. But Raegan was a sweet girl and a little naïve in general. It was hard not to like her.

After a lot of one-word answers and short questions, Ivan finally hung up the phone. "She's okay as far as Grant knows. He said he'll keep me updated."

"That's so scary," Dominique said, wrapping her arms around herself.

Next to her, Ruby looked as worried as he'd ever seen her. And he'd seen the beauty in a hospital room after nearly being hit by a car. She'd only sprained her ankle and suffered from a few cuts and bruises but he'd never forget seeing her there, injured. It had shaved years off his life, knowing that day could have been much worse. The maniac driving the car could have killed her and wouldn't have cared.

When she looked at him, he automatically looked away. Because yeah, he was a coward where she was concerned.

As everyone started talking about heading home, Ruby sidled up to him. It surprised him. "Give me a ride tonight?" she asked quietly.

For the briefest moment, his mind went where he swore to never let it. He'd love to give her a ride. Over and over. But he'd never have a shot with a woman like Ruby. Not with his jacked-up face. She was friends with his sister, had worked with Jules for years. He'd only ever met her a year ago for the first time though. Since then she'd consumed his fantasies. Which was just plain stupid. "Sure," he said instead, surprising himself.

She gave him a sweet smile, but there was a glimmer of...something in her eyes. Something he couldn't get a handle on because it looked a lot like sexual attraction. He'd seen her shoot down pretty much every guy who hit on her, including his younger brother. Jules always joked that Ruby made grown men cry. And Montez believed it.

Ruby looked like Marilyn Monroe. Blonde, curvy and walking sex. And damn she had a mouth on her. He loved the smart-ass stuff she was always saying to people. Tonight she had on one of those pinup-style dresses his sister sold at the shop Ruby ran with her. She looked like one of those women painted on World War II bomber planes. He wanted to peel the black and white thing off her, to slowly reveal every inch of her luscious body before he kissed all of her smooth skin. But that was a stupid, stupid thing to wish for.

They weren't even in the same league, and not just because he was fucked-up looking. Though that was a big part of it.

After everyone said goodbye to each other and his younger brother gave him a not-so-subtle thumbs up about taking Ruby home, they headed out. He wasn't sure what the hell Sandro thought would happen, but this was just a ride, plain and simple.

"Are you working tomorrow?" Ruby asked as he steered out of the parking lot. She crossed her legs so that she was turned toward him.

He got hard at just that flash of leg. Who was he kidding? He'd been hard practically all damn night watching her. Because simply watching her was addicting. The thought of actually touching her…nope, not going there.

"Yeah. Saturday nights are always busy." He owned and ran La Playa Grill. Had pretty much since he'd gotten out of the Marines. He might not have come back from his last combat tour whole, but he could cook and he knew numbers. Not to mention he'd grown up in his parents' restaurant. He knew what it took to make a restaurant successful. The right employees, enough startup capital and a lot of hard work. Mainly hard work.

"I'm surprised you were even out tonight."

He hadn't planned on coming at all. And he probably wouldn't have if he'd known she'd be there. Being around her hurt too damn much. Seeing what he could never have. But his brother had asked him, so he'd come. "Sandro begged me."

She snorted, laughing. "As a wingman for his fruitless quest to land Dominique, right?"

He shot her a quick glance, saw the laughter dancing in her eyes. "You would be right."

"He needs a woman to take care of him, but D isn't it."

"Why do you say that?"

"Which part?"

"Both."

"Well, your brother is the type of man who needs a woman to take care of him. Period. I blame your sweet mother for that."

Now he snorted because it was the truth. "*Dios*, my mama spoiled him."

"And he's not D's type. She wants a man to take charge of her."

Montez cleared his throat. This was the first time he and Ruby had ever been alone together and this was veering toward…interesting territory. He wondered if she wanted a man to take charge of her. It was hard to imagine, knowing what he did of her. "Yeah?"

"Not, like, financially, but you know…" She trailed off, her grin wicked. "In the bedroom."

"What type of woman are you?" The question was out before he could stop himself. He didn't want to know. Except even he couldn't make himself believe his own lie.

"I want a man who knows what he's doing in the bedroom. And…" For the first time since he'd known Ruby she actually looked vulnerable. She paused a little longer than was normal before continuing. "I want someone who can take charge. To dominate me." She said the last three words in a rush before looking out the window, away from him.

Shock threaded through him. Yep. His dick was never going to go down at this rate. Different responses were on the tip of his tongue, but he couldn't voice any of them. His throat was too tight. All he could imagine was tying Ruby down, pleasuring her with his mouth as she came on his tongue, as he tasted her pleasure. He'd never pictured her as the type of woman to let herself lose control.

He shifted uncomfortably as he drove through the bright streets of Miami. Even this late, the city was alive, pulsing with energy. Some places would be quiet, especially the older, more established neighborhoods, but Ruby had a townhome in one of the newest parts of the city.

They weren't that far from the club, about twenty minutes. Her townhome was in an area that neighbored a shopping center complete with a Target and locally owned boutiques. It also wasn't far from where she worked with Jules.

"My car is in the garage but you can park in the driveway..." She blinked suddenly, her eyes narrowing at him as he put his truck in park. "How the hell do you know where I live?" she demanded, shifting away from him until she was practically against the door.

The flash of fear he saw in her eyes stunned him. "I brought you food before, when you hurt your ankle. Jules gave me the address. I swear." The streak of terror rolling off her slashed at him even as it surprised him. He wanted to reach out, to comfort her, but sensed it wouldn't be welcome.

She pushed out a harsh breath, raked a shaky hand through her hair. "Of course, I'm...jeez, I'm sorry. I just, I was stalked by this guy once. It freaked me out. Wait...you're the one who brought me all that food?"

"Yeah." He slid out of his seat as he answered. He didn't want to talk about that. And even if they weren't dating, he was still walking her to the door. And he was going to go back to that stalking thing.

"Why didn't you ever say anything?" she asked as he opened her door for her.

Of course she wouldn't let it drop. He shrugged.

She smacked his shoulder as they walked to her front door. "That's not a good enough answer. I'm going to need some actual words here."

"I don't know, I figured you knew it was me." Which was a lie. He'd just wanted to do something nice for her but he hadn't wanted her thanks or anything. She'd been injured and...he couldn't even think about what might have happened to her. He knew she'd assumed it was his parents or one of his siblings and he'd never felt the need to correct her.

"Well I didn't. I would have said something." She dug out her keys and slid one into the lock. "Want to come in for a drink? I'm still kinda wired after tonight. I won't sleep until I hear from Jules that Raegan is really okay."

Montez knew he should say no. But... "Yeah, okay." He already had a feeling he'd regret staying, but he couldn't leave her now. He hadn't had any alcohol tonight

so a beer or whatever would be fine. Once they were inside he looked away as she turned off her alarm system.
"You had a stalker?" That better be past tense too, because
if someone was bothering Ruby, they wouldn't be for
long.

"Yeah. It was years ago." Sighing, she motioned that
he should follow her down a short hallway. Her place was
bright and colorful and even smelled like her. A sort of
vanilla and something, maybe cinnamon, that always reminded him of Ruby surrounded him here.

It was hard not to stare at her ass as she walked. And
it was really hard not to wonder what she'd meant about
being dominated. He wasn't into kink, but the thought of
having Ruby all to himself... He rolled his shoulders once.
He needed to stop thinking about something that wasn't
going to happen.

"He killed himself," she continued. "Not that I'm happy
about it, but that's a former part of my life."

He could tell by her tone she didn't want to talk about
it so he didn't push. When they reached the kitchen she
flipped on the lights and slipped her heels off by the
kitchen entryway. Oh, hell, he should have done the same
earlier. "You want me to take my shoes off?"

Laughing, she shook her head and made a beeline for
the refrigerator. "Don't worry about it. Tomorrow's my
cleaning day. I don't care about the floors right now.
That's crazy about Raegan," she said, pulling out a beer
and a bottle of water.

When she handed the beer to him, he realized her
hand was shaking.

Well hell, she was really shaken up still. Of course. He hadn't even thought about that. In Afghanistan he'd seen more than his share of death. Had killed men and seen his own friends killed. Tonight sucked for Raegan but it didn't even register on his scale of screwed-up shit. Going against his self-preservation instinct, he took both drinks, put them on the nearest counter and pulled her into a hug. Seeing her shaken like this made all his protectiveness kick into high gear.

To his surprise she practically lunged at him, wrapping her arms around him tight. "I had a friend in high school who was roofied at a party. She wasn't as lucky as Raegan." Her whole body shook so he wrapped his arms tighter around her.

Tried not to notice how good she smelled. Or how amazing she felt pressed up against him. Her breasts were full, more than a handful. And he felt like a total dick for noticing. "I'm sorry."

She shook her head, her face tucked against his chest. "Tonight was just a reminder how careful we've always gotta be." Her voice was a little muffled.

"People suck," he muttered. He couldn't comprehend the need that some people had to hurt others, to violate them. But it permeated the world. That entitled, bullshit behavior.

"Yeah, no kidding." Her voice was soft as she pulled back, but only enough so that she could look up at him. Her eyes were wide as she watched him, and there was more than a hint of lust there.

The sight made something shift inside him. She'd had a few drinks tonight and she was clearly feeling vulnerable. He didn't want to take advantage of her but he'd give his left arm for a kiss. Just a taste.

"We got some new naughty nurse costumes at the store," Ruby murmured, her gaze dropping to his mouth.

He swallowed hard. How the hell was he supposed to respond to that? She shifted slightly against him and yep, came right in contact with his erection. He barely bit back a groan. It was impossible to hide. Now that he was holding her, touching her? No way it was going down anytime soon. Thinking about baseball or anything else wouldn't matter because Ruby was in his arms. That meant he was going to stay hard.

"They come in two different styles," she continued, her eyes locked onto his mouth, clear hunger there.

All he could do was stare at her beautiful face.

Now her gaze snapped up to meet his. "I was thinking I could model them for you, see which one you like better." Her voice was low, sultry and a mix of emotions bled into her gaze.

He couldn't get a read on any of them. He just knew that whatever this thing was, it wouldn't last. After getting burned before, literally and figuratively, he knew what his limits were. He could only offer her one thing. "Ruby…"

"Don't give me some song and dance about how you're Jules's brother and this can't happen. I know you want me." But she didn't sound sure. If anything, the confident woman he'd known the past year looked almost vulnerable.

That had to be bullshit though. She was perfect. "Of course I want you," he growled. "But I don't have anything to offer you other than sex. Just straight fucking and no promises of anything else. It'll be good, that I can promise, but nothing else will ever happen between us." He knew the words were crude, harsh, but this gave her an out.

Maybe she wanted to sleep with him, but he knew she wouldn't be proud to have him on her arm out in public. His ex-girlfriend had made that clear when he came back with a screwed-up face. He was good enough to sleep with but not to take out in public. Things between him and Ruby would only ever be physical. He hated it, but he was a realist. He could lay things out early so that he didn't get hurt, so that—

She stepped away from him, hurt etched into every line of her face. "Lock the door on your way out." Her voice was soft, too soft, as she walked out of the kitchen. He wished she'd have slapped him or…something else instead.

Fuck him. He gritted his teeth, rubbed a hand over his face. The feel of his damaged skin, the way he looked, was the only thing that kept him from going after her.

He shouldn't even be alive. He shouldn't have been the one to come home. Not when so many of his friends had been husbands, fathers. He didn't deserve Ruby. He didn't deserve anyone. Some days he thought the scarring on his face was his punishment for returning home alive. A constant reminder that he should have died in that desert.

So he left the way he'd come, locking the bottom handle of the front door before he pulled it shut behind him.

CHAPTER FOUR

Raegan felt as if she was coming out of a haze or a fuzzy dream in which nothing made sense. She could remember parts of it, but everything was cloudy.

"You sure she's gonna be okay?"

She blinked at the sound of male voices...Ford's voice. He was talking to someone in scrubs. A man. A doctor. They were at a clinic, not a hospital.

Why was he with her... She remembered now. The doctor—Dr. Hernandez—put this oxygen mask on her in case she had respiratory distress. He'd also taken her blood, given her something called activated charcoal and had kept her talking. She vaguely remembered Ford talking to her and sitting next to her, holding her hand. He'd been constantly by her side, she was pretty sure. She thought he'd told her she was drugged, maybe roofied? She couldn't remember though. She actually couldn't remember much of what she'd said at all. Or what he'd said. It was like there was a block in place, preventing her from remembering anything.

Which was scary.

"I'm sure. According to her blood work, the dosage was very low. You'll need to stay with her tonight." The doctor glanced at his watch, frowned. "Well, this morning. But she's showing no signs of respiratory distress, no convulsions and she hasn't been nauseous except when she first arrived. You'll need to watch her to make sure she doesn't get sick when she sleeps, but at this point there's nothing else I can do. It's been five hours and her symptoms are improving. She's okay to go home."

She pulled her oxygen mask down. "I've been here five hours?" An iciness slid through her. She couldn't believe she'd lost that much time.

Ford swiveled to her and hurried across the small room. He sat on a short, round stool next to her, his expression pure concern. "How are you feeling?"

"Okay. I think. What…happened again?" She was glad to have him by her side. Everything about him was solid, comforting.

His brow furrowed. "You don't remember anything?"

"A little. I remember leaving for a club with my friends and…I remember you and Doctor Hernandez asking me a lot of questions and keeping me talking." Even if she couldn't remember what she'd said. She could feel her cheeks warming up as she worried about what she might have inadvertently confessed. She'd never done drugs so she wasn't sure if she would have blurted out stuff. Oh no—what if she'd admitted how much she wanted him?

"That's normal." The doctor came to stand on the other side of the bed, his expression gentle. He sat on a rickety-looking plastic chair. "You were given a very small dose of…the street term is GHB. You were very lucky."

Feeling sluggish, she turned to Ford. "You thought it was Rohypnol though, right?" Or maybe she'd imagined that conversation.

He nodded. "Yeah. GHB is pretty much the same thing though. Someone likely put it in your drink. In liquid form it's odorless and a little salty. So your drink likely covered up the salt taste."

"My drink… Are my friends okay?" She hated that she couldn't remember much about the night. There was music, laughter, dancing…bright lights. Somewhere near the beach.

"They're okay and they're worried about you. I've been in contact with a woman named Jules and with Grant."

"Julieta's so sweet," she murmured. "Wait, Grant came out with us?" That didn't sound right.

"No, but he knows what's going on."

"Oh, good, I guess. Why are you here?" Because she couldn't imagine what would have made him come out with her and her friends. It didn't even make sense.

"I was at the same club you were. Work thing. Purely by chance, saw some guy dragging you outside. He ran off and I couldn't leave you by yourself."

As the reality of his words set in, she shivered, wrapped her arms around herself. She was glad she was still in her own clothes and not scrubs. If Ford hadn't been there she could be in a hospital right now for a very different reason. A tremble racked her body and she couldn't stop it.

Ford took one of her hands, pulled it against his chest. His hold was steady, comforting. "You're okay. Something could have happened, but it didn't. And this isn't your fault. In the next few days and weeks you're going to second-guess yourself, berate yourself over 'letting' someone put something in your drink. Don't. You did everything right. You were with friends and shit just happened. An asshole drugged you and it wasn't your fault. And...I know it doesn't feel like it. But you're lucky." There was an understanding in his gaze, as if he knew what could have happened to her. Considering he was a cop, he'd probably seen the worst of humanity.

His expression and kind words broke something free inside her and to her horror, tears started rolling down her cheeks. Oh, God. This was pretty much the exact opposite of how she imagined spending time alone with Ford. It wasn't even in the same galaxy as her fantasies. He'd had to save her from being drugged and probably assaulted, maybe worse. At the very least, robbed. Now his Friday night had been spent at a clinic with her. This definitely wouldn't make him see her in a different light. Okay, that wasn't true. He probably thought she was a complete mess.

"Don't cry, sweetheart." His voice was deep, soothing as he pulled her into a hug and rubbed a big, steady hand down her spine.

She hitched in a breath at the word sweetheart, her tears drying up. That wasn't the first time he'd called her that, was it? She vaguely remembered... *Oh no!* She pulled back from him, wiping at her wet cheeks. "Did I kiss you?"

His neck flushed red and he did a weird shake then nod of his head. As if he couldn't decide whether to tell her the truth. But it was so obvious.

Ohmygodohmygodohmygod. That had been real. She remembered basically attacking him. Then him easing her back. She covered her face with her hand. It was official.

Tonight couldn't get any worse. "Can I go soon?" she mumbled.

"Yes," Dr. Hernandez said, his voice sympathetic. Which made her feel even crappier. "And Ford is right. None of this is your fault. I've started a file for you and I'm keeping a record of your blood work, but...you weren't assaulted. Someone dosing you with an illegal substance against your knowledge is a felony but unless the police catch who did this I don't know that my records will matter."

She'd rather have everything documented, regardless. "I...have insurance. I don't think I have my card with me though. Do I even have my purse?" Now panic punched through her. Her credit cards, her driver's license—

"I've got it. And your phone," Ford said.

"Don't worry about paying me. Make a donation to the clinic later," the doctor said in a tone that made it clear this wasn't up for discussion.

"Okay. Thank you." She laid her head back against the flat pillow typical of medical places. She waited while Ford and the doctor talked quietly again, out of earshot, then she waited more as the doctor came back and talked to her again, going over everything one more time.

When it was time to leave, she wasn't surprised that Ford wrapped an arm around her shoulders, steadying her, but having the huge, sexy guy so close was jarring to her senses nonetheless. "I've already talked to your cousins. Porter wants me to bring you to his and Lizzy's place. They want—"

"No. I'm just going to go home. They have a one-year-old. They don't need me there interrupting them in the middle of the night." And she was embarrassed. Right now she wanted to be alone.

The humid, salt-tinged air rushed over her as they stepped out into the dimly lit parking lot. They must not be far from the beach if she could still smell it.

He didn't respond, just frowned at her. She turned away. She wasn't going to bother her cousin and his wife, and she didn't care what Ford said. There were two vehicles in the parking lot. One was a truck she was fairly certain belonged to him.

Sure enough, he led her to the truck, opened the passenger-side door for her. The action was so sweet, reminding her of where she'd grown up. Aaaand she remembered kissing him the last time she was sitting in here. Her cheeks burned with embarrassment but she shoved the thought away and got inside. Once she was alone she'd wallow in mortification at the way she'd attacked him.

Once he slid into the driver's seat he turned the ignition on but didn't make an attempt to leave. "Look. You shouldn't be alone right now."

"I'm not going to Porter's." *Ugh.* She knew she was being stubborn, but she'd worked hard to get her independence. The thought of heading over there now at almost three in the morning? Just no. She didn't want to do it.

"I was going to say you could stay with me for the next few hours, get some sleep. In the morning, or later this morning, I can take you home. So either my place or Porter's—or your place. But if you go home, you know Porter will just drag you up to his condo, probably using guilt. So your choice." There was no give in his voice.

"Your place." She should have just said Porter's, because putting Ford out like this was probably taking advantage of him. But something told her he wouldn't make the offer if he didn't mean it. And okay, she wanted to be with him right now. She felt like a total mess and this man made her feel safe. She didn't care what that said about her. And he was right. If she went home, Porter or Lizzy—or probably both—would insist she come upstairs to their condo or just plant themselves in her place. "Only if you don't mind."

His eyes dipped to her mouth for a long, heated moment. "I don't mind," he rasped out, looking away from her before kicking the truck into drive.

She blinked in surprise. What the heck had that just been? Did Ford...*want* her? Raegan was still a little fuzzy on some things but she was pretty sure that had been a healthy dose of lust she'd just seen.

Well that was...interesting. And very, very welcome.

* * *

Damn it, damn it, damn it.

He slammed his fist into the punching bag in one of his extra bedrooms. He'd set it up as a personal gym instead of a bedroom. He had to stay fit.

In middle school he'd been picked on, bullied. Nothing he could ever tell his father about because he had to be tough. He'd gotten tough, all right. By high school he'd been in track and ripped. No one picked on him again.

Now he still worked out, kept his body perfect. He wasn't bulked up though. No, he was all lean muscle.

Something Raegan would appreciate when he finally got her alone.

He'd hinted that he might want to take her out, but she'd laughed it off. As if the very idea was hilarious. It wasn't as if he wanted for pussy. He got pretty much whoever he wanted when he went out.

But he wanted Raegan. He would have her.

Tonight she'd been so out of it, hadn't even seemed to recognize him. She was his. He'd do whatever he wanted. He hadn't wanted to hurt her though. Just make sure she understood she belonged to him. Then that guy had shown up. He'd seen him before...somewhere.

Frowning, he stopped, stilled the swinging punching bag. He had seen that guy. But where?

Grabbing a towel, he wiped the sweat off his face and neck before heading to his office. One wall had a display of pictures of Raegan. She had no idea he took them. No one did.

He scanned the pictures, didn't see anyone in the background who looked like the guy from the club.

But these were of her anyway. He'd made sure to only put up images of her or mostly her, cutting out anyone who might be in the background.

He pulled out a box of extra photos, the ones that didn't make it to the Wall of Raegan. After twenty minutes of flipping through pictures, he found one with the guy in it. The picture had been taken outside Grant Caldwell's house.

He'd followed Raegan there once, hadn't realized who the home belonged to until later. He'd taken pictures of

SECRET OBSESSION | 51

everyone coming and going from some party. A barbe-que-type thing. He tapped his finger against the guy's face. He might not know his name, but this guy knew Grant or at least worked for Red Stone.

Though…he didn't remember seeing the guy at Red Stone. Maybe he was just friends with Raegan's cousin.

Or maybe he was fucking Raegan.

Rage surged through him at that thought but he quickly shoved it back down. No.

He refused to believe that. She wasn't seeing anyone. He'd know. And she hadn't shown up with that guy to-night. And no man, not if he was Raegan's boyfriend, would let her go out with a bunch of friends. Especially not dressed like she'd been.

Her dress had been bright, revealing. As if she wanted attention.

She'd certainly gotten his.

He didn't want anyone else to look at her though. Once she was his, he'd make sure she understood that she couldn't dress like a whore.

He closed the box and slid it back into a drawer, but he kept out the picture of the man who'd interrupted him.

"I'm going to find out exactly who you are," he said, tracing an X over the guy's face.

Tonight would have been perfect if not for this bas-tard. He'd gotten in his and Raegan's way. That was un-acceptable.

CHAPTER FIVE

For a long moment Raegan looked around the unfamiliar, masculine bedroom. Panic spread through her until she remembered where she was.

Ford Burke's house.

In his bed.

Wearing one of his T-shirts.

After a very terrifying night. *Ugh.* It tasted like something had died in her mouth and she had a wicked headache.

Everything was still pretty fuzzy but she remembered Ford bringing her back to his place. She'd tried to insist on sleeping on the couch but he'd pretty much run over her arguments in a few seconds flat. She'd have never agreed to come to his place if she'd known he didn't have another bed. He had another room, but it was an office. She couldn't worry about that now.

After washing her face and brushing her teeth in his bathroom, she found him in the kitchen.

Cooking.

It was probably one of the sexiest things she'd ever seen. He had on a pair of jeans and nothing else. His broad back practically begged for her to run her fingers over all those carved lines. Something was sizzling at the stove and whatever it was, it smelled delicious.

"How're you feeling?" he asked without turning around.

Feeling guilty at being caught staring—and how had he even known she was there?—she nearly jumped. "Um, good, thanks. I used your toothbrush," she blurted. She felt bad about doing it, but she couldn't face the idea of seeing him this morning with breath like a garbage can. "I'll buy you a new one."

Laughing in clear surprise, he glanced over his shoulder to pin her with a sensual look. "That's okay. I've got extras."

She didn't know what to do about that look, was feeling way too out of sorts after last night. She knew what he'd told her had happened, but she didn't even remember being taken out of the club by some guy and she barely remembered the five hours at the clinic. Only after was clearer. "Thanks. I just...I felt really gross. Thanks again for letting me stay over. I know what a big inconvenience this is."

He just snorted, which could have meant any number of things.

"I, uh, I was just going to call a taxi and get a ride back to my place but I'm not sure where my phone is." And she hated the thought of heading home in her club dress and heels.

Flipping off the stove, he slid the pan off the burner before turning to her. "First, you're going to eat." He nodded at the rectangular table next to a window that overlooked a neat backyard with an S-shaped pool. It glistened under the bright morning sunlight. "Then I'll take you wherever you want to go."

She wasn't sure how she felt about taking orders, but there was no reason to argue when he was just looking out for her and was possibly one of the sweetest men she'd ever met. And food sounded really good. Wishing she'd put on sweatpants or something other than the long T-shirt that came to mid-thigh, she sat at the table. "Do you need help with anything?"

"Nope." He moved around the kitchen like a pro, which, again, was ridiculously sexy.

"Have you talked to Grant or Porter this morning?" *Please say no*, she thought.

"I talked to all of your cousins. Keith too."

She cringed. Crap. Her uncle was even more protective than his sons. "I'm a little surprised they're not here. They can be total cavemen." Because she could actually see them storming over to Ford's place like lunatics. They were normally sane, well-trained security guys who ran a multi-million dollar company—or maybe billion, she wasn't sure. But they could act like big kids sometimes. She just hoped Belle had a son, for Grant's sake. And their future child's sake. She couldn't even imagine how nuts they'd all be if Belle had a little girl.

"They wanted to come over." There was something in his voice, an edge almost, that did something strange to her insides.

Not many people could tell her relatives to back off—and actually have them listen. Another point on the Ford sexiness scale. The guy was pretty much off the charts by now. She wondered what he looked like in uniform. She figured that was the last thing she should be thinking about but it was hard not to be curious—and fantasize.

"I've never seen you in your uniform," she murmured as he brought her a plate of eggs, bacon and toast. She wasn't sure why she'd said it out loud. Apparently she didn't have a filter this morning. She'd blame it on the drugs.

He lifted a big shoulder. She tracked it with her gaze, suddenly feeling just a bit warmer. "I don't wear it often. Mainly for funerals or a mandatory event. Coffee?"

She nodded. "Cream and sugar. And, seriously, thanks again. You don't have to do all this." She felt bad just sitting there while he waited on her. It was disconcerting.

"I want to." The words came out pointed.

And she didn't know what to do with that. She was still feeling out of sorts simply by being in his kitchen, his house, alone with him. This was one of those surreal situations she'd never planned on being in. Of course, no one planned on getting drugged and almost assaulted.

Against her will a shudder streaked down her spine. If she let herself think about what could have happened last night she was pretty sure she'd have a breakdown. A blank space in her memory was terrifying. She couldn't remember the face of the man who'd tried to take her away from her friends. She could have woken up this morning somewhere else and… Her stomach roiled as her mind filled in a dozen different scenarios. Before she realized it, Ford was crouched in front of her.

"You okay?" God, he watched her with such concern in those beautiful green eyes.

For the first time, she saw that he had little gold flecks in his eyes. She cleared her throat. "I'm just feeling really stupid right now," she whispered, a chill overtaking her despite the even temperature in the room and the sun-light streaming through the windows, bathing her and the table.

His frown deepened. "Stupid?"

She nodded once, her throat tight. "From the time I was fourteen I've pretty much known the things I have to do to watch out for myself. Watch my drinks, don't go to parties with boys or men you don't know. Always have a buddy no matter what, especially if you're at a club. Meet up for dates in public places, don't let anyone pick you up from your house unless you really know him. Stuff like that. I just, God, I want to kick myself—"

His mouth was suddenly on hers, soft and sweet and, okay, a little bit demanding.

Even though she was surprised, she didn't question it, just leaned into him. Because of the way he was crouched, they were practically at eye level. She dug her fingers into his shoulders, moaned into his mouth. It was hard to be-lieve she was kissing Ford but if last night was the crap-piest night she'd ever had, this was the best morning because holy hell, the man could kiss.

He let out a low, almost growling sound as he slid one hand through her hair and cupped the back of her head. Now she was really glad she'd brushed her teeth. His hold was dominating, sexy and she felt it all the way to her toes.

He tasted like coffee and cinnamon. Maybe his fla-vored creamer. Whatever it was, she wanted to bottle it up because he tasted like heaven. The subtle scent of his cologne or body wash teased her, wrapped around her and she knew the smell was permanently imprinted in her brain. Everything about Ford was absolutely delicious.

When he flicked his tongue against hers, teasing, taking, she started to slide off her chair, wanting to get closer to him.

Wanting to get totally naked with him.

Yeah, she knew it was way too soon, but it was hard to care. The attraction she felt for Ford was off the charts crazy. The first time she'd met him it had been a punch to all her senses. She'd wondered if maybe it was because she'd been relatively sheltered growing up, but nope—since moving to Miami she'd met plenty of men.

No one got her turned on the way Ford did. She could hardly believe he was kissing her, clearly wanted her. He'd been so standoffish in the past.

When he pulled back, she made a little protesting sound. She didn't want to stop. Not now. Things were just getting good.

His big palms spanned her thighs as he clutched onto her. He laid his forehead against hers, his breathing erratic. "You need to eat."

She ran her fingers along his bare shoulders. He should never, ever wear shirts. "I need to kiss you again."

He half grinned, closed his eyes as if in pain, then stepped back. "Eat. You had a rough night. I don't...you just need to eat."

She wanted to tell him that food could wait, but he turned away from her and started making his own plate. Way too many emotions pummeled through her, but if he didn't want to kiss anymore she wouldn't beg him. Her stomach growled, as if on cue. Okay, maybe she *should* eat.

She wanted way more of what sexy Ford had to offer. He was impossible to read though. She wondered if he'd kissed her just to shut her up. No...she could see that she very much physically affected him. No way for him to hide his erection.

Not that he seemed to be trying.

So why did he stop? Under different circumstances she might have questioned him, but she needed food, a shower and her own clothes. And to call her friends, let them know she was okay. Not to mention her family. It didn't matter that Ford had already talked to them—she needed to let her cousins and her uncle know she was totally unharmed.

But she knew he wouldn't have kissed her unless he was interested. She'd ask him about it. Eventually.

* * *

Ford wasn't sure what had come over him, kissing Raegan like that. Okay, he knew exactly what had come over him. She was under his skin.

And he knew that wasn't going to change anytime soon.

"Thanks again for taking me home," she murmured as they pulled into the private parking garage at her building.

He knew Porter was renting one of his condos to her, was glad she lived somewhere so safe. "You don't have to keep thanking me." It made him uncomfortable. He'd helped her the way he'd have helped any woman. Okay, he'd gone a little beyond what he normally would have done by letting her stay over.

"Fine, I'll try not to." Her voice was light, a little teasing. "Did you tell Porter we were coming here?" she asked.

"No." He'd decided not to for purely selfish reasons. He wanted to spend more time with Raegan. And if her cousin knew she was in the building, he'd take the elevator down to see her.

She let out a sigh of pure relief. "Thank God. He seemed fine when I talked to him earlier but I have a feeling he's going to go into lockdown mode and try to keep me close to home."

That wasn't a bad idea, but Ford didn't say anything. It was common enough in clubs for assholes to drug random women. Sometimes men just drugged whoever they could, with no intention of assaulting any particular woman. Of course that didn't mean the woman wasn't hurt by some other asshole taking advantage of a situation. He'd seen enough of that shit when he'd been on patrol. Just because it was likely Raegan had been a target of pure convenience didn't mean he wasn't going to follow up. He'd already put in a call to the club's owner and apparently so had Keith Caldwell.

Considering Keith was respected—and feared—in pretty much every circle, Ford had a feeling getting the security feeds from that place was going to be easy. "What are your plans for today?" He hated that he couldn't insist she take it easy and stay home. But he had no right. She wasn't his.

Even though he wanted her to be.

"I want to stop by Julieta's—that's the friend you talked to. She owns a little boutique and runs it with another friend, Ruby, who was there last night too. I just want to see them in person. Jules sounded pretty torn up when I talked to her. I think she feels guilty."

"Sometimes shit just happens," he said, parking when she pointed to a numbered spot.

"No kidding."

He had a feeling she'd have to keep reminding herself of that over the next couple weeks. A scare like this would make her question herself and everyone around her, at least for a little while. He wished he could be around to protect her from...everything.

"This must be what it's like to do the walk of shame," she muttered, looking down at her clothes. Raegan had on a T-shirt and sweatpants she'd borrowed from him.

They were too big, but he liked the sight of her in his clothes. Something he didn't plan to analyze too closely. He laughed at her words. "I wouldn't know."

Her hand on the door, she half smiled. "Me neither. I just hope no one from my floor sees me like this."

"You're a grownup. They'll get over it if they do."

She grinned at his words and slid from his truck at the same time he did. "I didn't notice it before, but seriously, you're driving a Ford truck?"

"I can't drive a Chevy or anything else, not with my name," he said, rounding the hood to meet her.

She motioned toward the east side of the parking garage. "Elevators are at the end of this aisle, around the corner. How did your parents come up with the name Ford anyway?"

He shot her a sideways glance as they headed across the quiet garage. He knew the security here was good, but he automatically scanned for any threats. After what had happened to her, he was feeling particularly vigilant. "Guess," he said.

"Don't tell me it's because you were conceived in one?" Her eyes widened slightly.

He wished he could say no. "Yep. I'm just glad my name's not Mustang."

She snorted as they reached the elevators. "That's pretty awesome. Is it just you?"

"I have a brother." Who he didn't want to talk about. Or think about. He rolled his shoulders once as she swiped her access card against the security pad.

"What's with the tone?" She glanced up at him, her expression curious.

"There's no tone." She was just good at reading him, apparently. It surprised him a little, but it was easy to let his guard down around her.

Her very pretty lips quirked up as the elevator dinged softly, the doors whooshing open. "You're definitely lying but since I'm wearing your clothes and you saved me last night, I'll let it slide."

He loved the way she was with him, with people in general. In their past interactions he'd noticed that she had a way about her that put people at ease. Everything about her was so real, and in a sometimes plastic city, it was refreshing. "So if I hadn't saved you, you wouldn't let me off the hook?"

"Pretty much." She gave him a full-on smile and his heart rate kicked up to epic proportions. "You're from here, right?"

"Yeah, born and raised in Homestead, then later I moved to Miami when I got a job with the PD." He'd also been in the Corps in between those years but didn't bring it up.

"I heard from a little birdie that Grant keeps trying to get you to work for Red Stone," she said as the elevator doors opened onto her floor.

"Ever since he went to the dark side he's been trying to bring me with him." Grant had been a detective before going to work with his family at Red Stone Security.

She nudged him with her hip. "Hey, I work for said dark side. And the benefits are great in private security."

Grinning, he shook his head. "I like my job."

"Good. This is me," she said as they came to stand in front of a door halfway down the plush hall. "You...want to come in for a coffee? You don't have to," she rushed out.

He'd just planned to make sure she got to her door safely, but there was something in her expression that looked a little like fear. Which made sense. After last night, of course she was probably feeling scared. He nodded. "Yeah."

Blushing prettily, she opened the door and he followed after her.

When he didn't hear the telltale beeping sound of an alarm, he frowned. "Don't you have a security system?"

"Yes, but I was running late yesterday and forgot to set it. The building is ridiculously secure though, so it's fine—what's that look?"

He lifted a shoulder, trying to remain casual. Every protective instinct inside him was pretty much ordering him to do a full sweep of her place. Just in case. He knew it was crazy because she was right—the building was one of the most secure in the city. But logic didn't play into his need to protect Raegan.

"You totally want to check out my place right now, don't you? To make sure it's secure."

"Maybe."

She gave him a slightly wondering look. "You really are cut from the same cloth as my cousins." Surprising him, she motioned down the hallway with her hand, a grin tugging at her lips. "Go for it."

Not caring that he'd ventured into complete overprotective mode, he did just that, quickly sweeping her one-bedroom place. He found her in the kitchen, pulling two bottles of water from the stainless steel refrigerator. "Is my home free of burglars?" she asked, handing him a bottle.

"You're good to go." Of course, now that he'd seen her bedroom, a place he'd fantasized about, all he could think about was her lying in it. Naked. Under him or on top of him, it didn't matter.

"Good. And I know you said to stop thanking you, but whatever, I'm doing it again. Thank you for this. I...was a little scared to come home by myself, which feels stupid, but..." Trailing off, she shrugged.

"It's not stupid," he murmured, his gaze dipping to her mouth even as he told himself not to. After that kiss in his kitchen, the memory of her taste and the sweet way she'd moaned into his mouth had been replaying over and over in his mind.

She cleared her throat, almost nervously. "So...after running up to Julieta's shop this morning I was going to head to the beach for a couple hours. Do you want to come with me? No pressure if you can't, I—"

"I'd love to." The words were out before he could stop himself. He hadn't been to the beach for relaxation in as long as he could remember. But getting to spend more time with Raegan, and seeing her in a bathing suit? Yeah. Even if he knew he was playing with fire, he couldn't seem to make himself walk away from her. For once, he made himself ignore the voice in his head that told him things would end badly, that he'd just end up getting burned again.

CHAPTER SIX

"**A**re you trying to destroy my new shipment?" Ruby looked up to find Julieta frowning at her. With a box cutter in one hand and pieces of a destroyed cardboard box on the ground around her, Ruby figured she probably looked a little nuts. "I already took the clothes out."

"So you just decided to attack a poor, defenseless box?" Julieta lifted an eyebrow, her lips curving up into an amused grin as she looked at the tattered remains littering the otherwise clean floor.

"I'm in a bitchy mood today, sorry." She figured she might as well be honest. Well, as honest as she could be. She certainly wasn't going to tell Julieta that her oldest brother was a big jerk who she wanted to punch in the face right now.

Immediately Julieta's expression morphed to one of concern. "I'm feeling weird about last night too. Raegan's on her way over though. She just called. That cop who helped her is with her."

Ruby's mood lifted a fraction. She set the box cutter down on the table they used for unloading. "Is this the same guy she's had a thing for since moving to Miami?"

"I don't know. She was cagey on the phone."

"Well if he's coming with her..." For months, Raegan had had a crush on some guy who her cousin Grant was friends with, but she'd never told them the guy's name. She'd been really private about it. Not that Ruby could exactly blame her. Ruby hadn't admitted to anyone she was half in love with Montez—because he was Julieta's brother. After last night though, she realized she needed to move on from him. It was clear nothing could ever happen between them.

"Yeah, I thought so too. And he knows Grant so I think it must be the same guy, because she told me Grant and Mystery Man used to work together."

At the buzzing sound, letting them know a customer had just entered the store, Ruby smoothed a hand down her red, scoop collar vintage-style dress. This was one of her go-to dresses when she was feeling crappy. "Do whatever it is you came back here to do. I've got the front."

"I'm hiding this box cutter and all knives," she called out as Ruby disappeared through the door to the front.

The laughter died on her lips when she saw Montez standing in the middle of the store. He looked out of place among all the displays of lingerie. Thankfully the sex toys were at the front of the shop in a discreet display case, but she didn't want to see him right now.

Not when she was still so hurt after last night. That's what she got for putting herself out there. She'd thought Montez was different. They'd been friends for months and...whatever. It didn't matter now. "I'll get your sister," she said, already turning back to the storeroom door.

"I came to see you."

She should have known, but nerves still skittered through her. Montez had been in here maybe once since Ruby had been working here. Sandro came in all the time, but that was because he was a huge flirt and liked to hit on all of Julieta's friends. Pasting on a fake but friendly smile she turned back around. She didn't want Julieta to know anything was wrong so she could pretend if she had to.

"Need help finding something? A dildo perhaps?" Her heels clicked against the smooth wood floor as she rounded the cash register to greet him. She might not want to talk to him, but she wasn't going to hide from him.

He rubbed a hand over the back of his neck, turned the injured side of his face away as he so often did. As if she gave a crap about his scars. Yeah, they were hard to miss since they covered half his face, but they didn't take away from who he was, how he'd gotten them. She knew he'd nearly died saving his friends and even though he hadn't saved all of them, he was the bravest man she'd ever known.

"I was a dick last night," he said.

At least he admitted it. "Yep. A big one." She was glad he seemed nervous. Served him right.

"I'm sorry. I shouldn't have talked to you like that. I...there's no excuse. I'm just sorry."

She looked into his dark eyes and realized he truly was sorry. But that didn't ease any of the pain in her chest. She'd had it bad for him for a year. Pretty much ever since she'd met him. He could be so sweet and kind, especially to his family. But he could also be a surly jerk. He'd just never been that way to her before. Until last night. He'd talked to her like she was nothing and it cut deep. "Fine. Apology accepted."

"Damn it, Ruby." Expression pained, he stepped closer, until only a foot separated them.

She could see the tension in every line of his incredible body. She knew he ran every day. Some mornings when she opened up the shop she'd see him jogging in the area, as if demons were chasing him. For all she knew, maybe they were. He worked, spent time with his family, and worked out. As far as she knew that was pretty much all he'd done the past couple years since getting out of the Marines.

But she'd seen the way he looked at her and had kept waiting for him to make a move. After she'd almost been hit by that car and avoided what could have been a much worse fate from a lunatic, she'd thought he'd finally make a move. She was an old-fashioned kind of girl and she'd wanted him to. But when it was clear he wouldn't, enough was enough. She'd decided to go for it. After last night, however, she just wanted to smack him. "I said, apology accepted."

His jaw tightened, pulling his scars tighter. "You're pissed at me."

"Of course I'm pissed!" She winced, glanced over her shoulder. The storeroom door was still closed and they didn't have any customers, but still, this was where she worked and she didn't want Julieta overhearing any of this. She turned back to face him. "You talked to me like I was a whore," she said quietly, rage surging through her. Last night she'd been too shocked to respond other than to tell him to leave. But now that he was standing in front of her she couldn't hold back.

He moved lightning fast until he was right in front of her. He reached out, grabbed one of her hips with his hand.

She blinked at the possessive grip, but also didn't step back. She hated that she liked the feel of him holding her.

"You're not a whore," he bit out, looking as pissed as she felt. "I was crude because I was... It doesn't matter. Fuck. I was wrong and I'm sorry. I didn't mean to talk to you like that or make you feel like that. Let me make it up to you, please."

"There's nothing you can do. I want more than sex, more than fucking." She whispered the last part, still angry at the way he'd spoken to her. "I won't settle for something less than I deserve, even if I am into you. I thought you were different, but last night—"

His fingers tightened. "Ruby—"

"No. You're just another asshole." She pushed at his chest as she heard the storeroom door opening. Almost at the same time the front door to the store opened and two women, sisters if she had to guess, came in laughing to each other.

Perfect timing.

Completely ignoring Montez, she sidestepped him and went to greet the customers. She hoped he'd leave because she had nothing left to say to him. Work was exactly what she needed when all she wanted to do was cry.

* * *

"What's that look?" Raegan asked, her beach bag hooked on her shoulder as Ford pulled out a towel and beach umbrella from the back seat of his truck. He was glad she'd asked him to come with her.

Ford's lips curved up at her question. His aviators hid his eyes but apparently she was learning to read him. Which was...interesting. She was more perceptive than some cops. "Nothing. Just thinking that it's been a long time since I've done this."

"Done what?"

"Gone to the beach."

She pushed her own sunglasses down, gave him a pointed look as he shut the door. "You live in Miami. That's wrong on so many levels."

He just snorted as they headed for the boardwalk. "Sand just reminds me of the desert." And he hadn't had a lot of fun there. Not to mention he always felt like a sitting duck on the beach. Which he knew was ridiculous. But there was literally no cover from an attack. Not that he expected to be attacked on South Beach, but some things had been ingrained in him long ago.

"Oh, right. Grant mentioned you were in the Marines too." She glanced at him. "Was it hard to transition back?"

He lifted a shoulder. That was a complicated answer and not one for a beach day. "I had it harder than some, easier than others."

She nudged him with her hip. "That's a very evasive answer."

He just grinned. Being around Raegan was a breath of fresh air. "Maybe I'll tell you more one day." The thought of opening up to anyone was hard enough, but especially a woman who he was starting to have real feelings for.

"I'm glad you came with me today."

SECRET OBSESSION | 73

"I am too." After their kiss this morning he'd been feeling unsettled. She hadn't brought it up and he wasn't going to either. Not yet anyway. "Your friends were nice."

"Thanks. I think Jules feels a lot better now after seeing me. Or she seemed to."

He nodded. It was clear both her friends had been experiencing a lot of guilt over last night.

"Ford?" A familiar male voice made him stop dead in his tracks. All the muscles in his body pulled taut at the sound of his brother calling his name. *Seriously? What the fuck?*

Raegan stopped with him and they both turned to watch Dallas, wearing board shorts and a T-shirt, heading toward them. His dark hair was a little longer than Ford's, but there was no mistaking they were related. Even though this was the last person he wanted to see, he forced himself to be civil even as annoyance surged through him. He was past anger, but that didn't mean he needed or wanted to see his brother. "Hey, Dallas."

"What are you doing here?" his brother asked, an iced coffee in hand.

"Public beach." He shrugged, not caring if he sounded like a dick.

"Oh yeah, I mean, I just...I'm surprised, is all. It's good to see you." He looked at Raegan, gave a nervous smile. "I'm Dallas, Ford's brother."

Raegan was all smiles as she shook his hand. "Raegan, Ford's friend."

He wanted to be more than friends, but right now, he just wanted Dallas gone. Being around his older brother brought up too much bullshit he didn't want to deal with.

Especially when he was with Raegan. He just wanted today to be about her.

"You guys here for the windsurfing thing?" Dallas continued when all Ford wanted to do was leave.

Ford had no idea what his brother was talking about. "No."

"Oh, well...I'm here with my new girlfriend." He motioned over to a blonde-haired woman in her thirties. The woman smiled at them. "She works for the firm. Another lawyer like me," he said, looking at Raegan, his smile polite. "If you guys want to join us—"

"We've got plans, but thanks for the offer." Yeah, Ford knew he was being an ass but he couldn't just stand around and pretend with Dallas.

"Right. Well...maybe I'll see you at Mom and Dad's next weekend?"

"Yeah, maybe." He avoided Sunday dinners when he knew Dallas would be there. Something his brother had to know.

"It was nice to meet you," Raegan murmured, hitching her bag slightly against her side.

"You too. Ford, I, uh, I'll see you around."

He didn't say anything as his brother left. "You want to grab a drink before we hit the sand?" he asked, turning back to Raegan.

"Um, no." She linked her arm through his as they continued down the boardwalk. He savored the unexpected closeness, even as he braced himself for the inevitable questions. "Is your brother a puppy murderer or something?"

He snorted. "No."

"Then what was that about? I know it's a super nosy question but I've never imagined you being so cold with someone."

"But you have imagined me in other scenarios?"

Now she snorted. "You're such a guy."

"That's not an answer." And he wanted to know if she had thought about him, fantasized about him. He might have been burned before but sweet Jesus he needed to let that shit go. If he wanted to move on, he knew he needed to deal with the past. He'd just never wanted someone enough to move on from that. And he sure as hell didn't want to think or talk about his brother anymore.

Even through his shades he could see her cheeks flushing red as they reached the sand. "You're deflecting from my question, but...fine, maybe I've thought about you in certain scenarios."

He bit back a groan. Maybe was good. "You feel like expanding on that?" he murmured, taking his shoes off as they started across the white sand beach.

"Nope. Two can play your game."

He sighed. "What do you want me to say?"

"I want to know what happened between you two. And also, was your brother conceived in Dallas?"

A laugh escaped before he could stop himself. "Sadly, yes."

"That's pretty awesome."

"Apparently he was conceived when they were there on a trip and my mom didn't want to name him after the hotel so she settled on the city instead."

"Your mom sounds fun."

A real smile lifted his lips. "Yeah, she is. Is this spot good?" He motioned to one of the only free strips of space on the packed beach. People with towels, coolers, radios and umbrellas were scattered out in every direction. That was another thing he didn't like about beaches—how crowded they were.

But when Raegan dropped her bag and stripped off her sundress he realized what a fool he was. Beaches were the best place on earth.

He swallowed hard, was glad for his sunglasses as he drank in the sight of her. Her bikini was plain black and showed off every inch of her body. From her full breasts to her slender waist and the soft flare of hips—he wanted to cover her up so no one else could see her. Which, she would say, was completely caveman of him.

She was of average height but because of her lean build and sexy-as-sin legs she seemed taller. Her legs were toned, slightly muscular, and he could imagine her wrapping them around his waist or shoulders as he buried his face between them.

Tearing his gaze away from her, he made himself busy with the umbrella. Anything was better than staring at her because he was having a difficult time keeping his reaction to her locked down.

Once the umbrella was in place he looked back at her to see that she was spraying on sunscreen and smoothing it over her arms and chest.

Scratch that, impossible.

He stripped off his shirt. "I'm gonna head to the water," he rasped out, unable to hide his erection.

Not only had he endured some of the toughest training in the world, he was now in his thirties. Not some randy teenager. But around Raegan none of that mattered.

It didn't matter that she was one of his best friend's cousins, or that she was a decade younger than him, or that he knew he'd likely get burned by her. He wanted to taste her again and this time he wasn't going to stop at kissing. Not unless she told him to.

CHAPTER SEVEN

Raegan didn't miss the looks a few women on the beach gave Ford as he practically stalked from her to the water. She wasn't sure what was going on with him but she also didn't blame people for looking at him. Heads popped up and swiveled, watching those long legs stride with purpose toward the ocean.

The man was a work of art. His physical appeal was part of it. There was no denying the man simply looked good enough to eat. He was all hard lines and raw sex appeal. But it was more than that. The way he carried himself was confident, clearly secure in who he was. That alone was damn sexy.

Earlier when he'd run into his brother he'd been different though. Not the secure man she knew. It had been so obvious his brother was trying to be nice and drag a conversation out of Ford. That had been a little strange and she couldn't deny that she was curious. But if he didn't want to talk about it, she wouldn't push.

After making sure her phone was tucked away in her bag, she zipped it up and headed to the water. The sand was warm against the soles of her feet, the sensation soothing. What had happened last night now felt a little surreal, almost like it had happened to someone else.

She just felt lucky that things hadn't been worse. And now here she was, hanging out with Ford. That was the best kind of silver lining she could imagine. When she stepped into the cool water, a sense of peace invaded her. Since moving to Miami she didn't think she would ever want to leave. For the first time in pretty much ever, she felt at home, like she belonged. She loved her parents and where she came from, but Miami was where she was supposed to be. She knew that bone deep.

"I have a confession to make," she said as she reached Ford. The water splashed around her waist as she moved farther out.

"Oh yeah?" His voice seemed a little deeper than normal and way more sensual.

Shivers skittered over her skin. "You're not the only one named after something." Or in her case, someone. "My mom had a crush on Ronald Reagan and named me after him. She apparently spelled my name wrong at the hospital and that's how I ended up with the 'e' and 'a' reversed."

His mouth curved up, sending another bout of butterflies off in her stomach. "Your name fits you."

"Thanks. Can I ask you something?" When he tensed she figured he thought she'd ask about his brother. But that was the last thing on her mind.

"Sure."

"Are we ever going to talk about that kiss?" Because she really, really wanted to. If she didn't remember how he'd tasted, how his lips felt against hers, that little groaning sound he'd made, she might have questioned whether it happened at all.

It was clear she surprised him. He scrubbed the back of his neck. Water rolled down from his arm, making soft splashing sounds. "I was worried that maybe I took advantage of you this morning."

Laughing lightly, she cut through the water so that only a foot separated them. She slid her sunglasses on top of her head so she could look at him and was glad when he did the same. She didn't want any barriers between them. "I liked it. A lot." Maybe that wasn't polished of her, to come out and say it, but she didn't care.

"I did too." His gaze dropped to her mouth, his eyes going heavy-lidded as he moved even closer. The water was clear enough today that she could see his hand moving toward her. When he loosely gripped one of her hips, she completely closed the distance between them.

And came right in contact with his erection as her body drew flush against his. She wasn't sure why she was surprised, but it shocked her a little. In the best way possible. There were a dozen or so people around them in the near vicinity but no one closer than thirty feet so they had plenty of privacy.

"I'd like to take you out. On a date," he added, as if to make it clear.

She had to squint a little because of the bright sunlight glinting off the Atlantic. "I'd like that too." Excitement danced out to all her nerve endings. She'd dated since moving to Miami, but she hadn't slept with anyone since...ugh, her sophomore year of college. Sex had just seemed overrated. Or more likely, she'd been with the wrong guys. Being this close to Ford, close enough to kiss him again, she had a strong feeling that sex with him would be incredible.

"Tonight?" he murmured, rolling his hips once against her.

Heat flooded between her legs. That sounded perfect. "Y—oh, I can't. I've got a stupid thing to go to. With a *friend*." And she hated that she'd agreed to be her friend's date. Part of her wanted to cancel, but that was a crappy thing to do to a friend. Plus, she'd promised.

For a moment his jaw tightened and she remembered that he'd been in her cousin's office when she'd told them she had that thing tonight. She wondered if they'd mentioned who she was going with.

Gah. "Tomorrow instead?" Because she didn't want to wait to go out with him.

His eyes were on her mouth again as he nodded and she felt that heated look all the way to her toes. "I'll pick you up around six?"

"Sounds good to me." Did it ever.

To her surprise, he leaned down, slowly, giving her time to back away if she wanted, but she had no intention of pulling back from sexy Ford.

For a brief moment, his lips skated over hers before he completely took control. He pulled her closer to him until their bodies collided while he slid his free hand through her hair, holding onto the back of her head.

Just like before she felt overwhelmed by him in the best way possible. Her palms settled against his chest as she leaned into him. She flicked her tongue against his, moaning into his mouth as his hand moved up, up, up, his big callused palm sliding up her waist and ribcage until he stopped just below her breast.

Her nipples ached and her entire body felt as if she was one giant exposed nerve. He didn't move any higher, but she could feel the tension humming through him, knew he wanted to touch her elsewhere.

Probably just as much as she wanted to touch him. But this was the beach and getting naked was definitely frowned upon.

Groaning softly, he pulled back, his breathing harsh, uneven. "I want to do more than kiss you right now." The words seemed to be torn from him as he watched her intently.

"Right back at you." She wanted to touch the man everywhere, get him worked up, see him lose total control.

But she'd heard anticipation was a good thing. It sure didn't feel like it though.

* * *

The beach was crowded today which wasn't a surprise. It was a beautiful, sunny Saturday in Miami. The perfect cover for what he needed to do.

He'd tracked Raegan here using her phone—which he'd cloned, since she'd been stupid enough to leave it lying out at work. It was like she wanted him in her life, watching her.

So far he'd just been intercepting her incoming messages and learning her schedule. He wanted to know everything about her. Where she went, who she hung out with. Copying her SIM card had been easy. But it wasn't enough.

He needed to be inside where she lived, to see where she slept at night. He'd tried to snag her keys a few times, but she always kept them locked up in her desk with her purse. But not her phone. She carried that everywhere. Cloning it had given him the perfect insight into her life, into who she really was. That was when he'd realized that they truly were perfect for each other.

That she was his. He started getting hard thinking about everything he wanted to do to her, so he shut off that train of thought.

When he saw her bag he knew she had to be nearby. Scanning the throng of beach chairs, people on towels, the bright rainbow of umbrellas fanning out along the white sand, he frowned. She had to be somewhere close. Stepping around a trio of umbrellas he continued looking—his throat constricted when he saw her in the water, kissing someone. Or he thought it was her. It was far away, maybe a hundred yards. But yeah, it was her. Raegan's long dark hair fell down her back as she pressed up against someone.

The man from the other night.

Stupid whore.

The man appeared to be holding onto her as if he owned her. No! She was his. None of her texts that he'd read had made it sound like she was with anyone. So this guy must be new.

He'd take care of the fucker soon enough.

Forcing himself to turn away, he moved back behind the umbrellas, using them as cover. He had on blue and white striped beach shorts, a T-shirt, a ball cap and jeans.

Standard gear for the beach. This morning, when he'd intercepted one of her texts to someone named Dominique, she'd told her friend that she was headed out to 'soak up some rays.'

He wanted to get a full view of her in a bathing suit, but she was too far out in the water. Which was just as well. She couldn't sneak up on him.

Acting as if he had every right to be digging in her bag, he quickly unzipped it and pilfered through it. *Damn it.* Other than extra clothes and a towel, he found only her phone, her ID and some cash in a zippered pouch. No keys.

Maybe the guy had her keys or maybe they were in the guy's vehicle. He couldn't be sure if she'd driven herself or come with the man.

Feeling as if someone was watching him, he looked up, scanned the surrounding area. A woman in a teal one-piece bathing suit had sunglasses on and was turned around in her beach chair, watching.

Or it looked as if she was watching him. It was impossible to tell with those sunglasses.

Even so, he'd already pushed his luck too much.

Standing unhurriedly, he moved away from the umbrella, bag and towels and headed back the way he'd come. Part of him wanted to stay, to watch, but he couldn't afford to be noticed.

Especially not after last night. For all he knew the man with her would remember him, would be able to identify him.

Not gonna happen. He'd been careful, had gotten to where he was in life because he was smart. He wouldn't start getting sloppy now.

Not when he was so close to claiming the prize.

CHAPTER EIGHT

"This is basically a glorified food and wine festival, isn't it?" Raegan asked her date, Rhys Martin Maxwell IV. She'd met him in Vegas during her first job with Red Stone—before her first and hopefully last kidnapping. They'd gone on a date and she'd quickly realized she had no attraction to him. He'd been okay with it after she'd told him she didn't want to go on another date with him.

But he'd wanted to stay friends so here they were, just friends. And he was always fun company.

"Yes. If I'm in town, I never miss it." He laughed lightly, his British accent faint and oh so proper sounding.

She didn't blame him, though she wished she was here with Ford—and felt guilty for even thinking that. Looking around the expansive outdoor setup, it was impressive. Twelve celebrity chefs were all manning various stations, cooking and talking to the guests, and gorgeous displays of food, wine and other cocktails were at various tables. Low-key music filtered in from speakers she couldn't see and there were always servers walking around with trays of drinks even with all the displays available. No one could possibly leave tonight hungry or thirsty.

Next to an owner/head chef of a local beach restaurant who was there for the celebration, a huge piece of driftwood had been hollowed out down the middle, filled with ice and bottles of blue champagne lining the entire thing. She was just glad the event wasn't formal. Most of the men were in slacks and button-down shirts and the women in cocktail dresses. Even with the misting fans and hidden coolers placed strategically around the space, it was still Florida in the summer. Getting overdressed would have made this miserable.

"Are you taking notes?" Rhys murmured, leaning down just a fraction. His cologne was crisp and masculine.

She turned to look at him, smiling. "Is it that obvious?" She was part of the new event planning department at Red Stone and couldn't help but be impressed by whoever they'd used for the setup tonight.

He gave her a half smile and briefly touched her bare shoulder. She'd worn a strapless black cocktail dress and heels. "You're looking sun-kissed."

"I went to the beach today." She stepped back just a fraction so that his hand dropped. She'd made it clear she just wanted to be friends and his touch wasn't unfriendly or creepy, but she just...wished it was Ford touching her. The man had gotten under her skin.

Rhys started to say something when Dominique appeared out of crowd, looking like a tall goddess. She'd left her long blonde hair down and had on a bright yellow dress that should have looked wrong with her hair color, but against her bronze skin and killer curves, she had most men and some women in the near vicinity turning to look at her. Which was pretty much standard for wherever Dominique went.

She smiled brightly when she spotted them, and to give Rhys credit, he didn't stare. Too hard. Not that Raegan cared if he did. Dominique was a beautiful woman, and Raegan and Rhys were just friends anyway.

"Athena said you were here," she said, swooping in with a hug and cheek kisses. She was five foot ten, but in her heels she was over six feet tonight and stunning.

"I'm still trying to decide where to start. All this food looks amazing." She motioned to Rhys, who was almost as tall as her friend. "Dominique, this is Rhys Maxwell."

After making introductions and brief small talk, Rhys said, "Champagne for you both?"

"Yes, thank you," Raegan said as Dominique nodded.

"Nice," her friend murmured once he was out of earshot. Just as quickly her expression morphed to one of concern. "I didn't want to say anything in front of him in case you hadn't told him, but...you're sure you're okay? I kinda can't believe you're here tonight."

She grasped Dominique's hand once before dropping it. "Thank you for not saying anything. And I'm fine, I swear. I've been fine since this morning. Just...weirded out." Raegan had already told her all this earlier in the day but she was glad her friend was concerned enough to ask again.

"Okay, well, you look fantastic."

"So do you. You're like a beach goddess."

Dominique just snorted. "So you're here with a sexy Brit but I heard from a reliable source that you were out this morning with a sexy cop. Spill everything."

"There's nothing to tell." *Not yet anyway.* "He's friends with Grant and...I don't know. We kissed and have a date tomorrow night." She felt her cheeks heat up even as she thought about the feel of Ford's lips against hers. For the tenth time tonight she wished she was out with him instead of here.

"That must have been some kiss. So you're really just friends with this one?" she asked, glancing over in the direction of Rhys, who was talking to a man Raegan had never seen before. Before she could respond, Dominique turned back to her, her jaw set tight. "I hate that man," she practically snarled, her cheeks flushing red.

The change in Dominique's composure was jarring. Raegan blinked. "The guy with Rhys?" Dominique simply nodded, as if talking was too much for her. She'd never seen her friend upset before. "Who is he?"

"Viktor Ivanov. He's a monster."

Concern punched through her. "Did he hurt you?"

She just snorted. "Please. He's the owner of the club we were at last night. I didn't find that out until today or I never would have gone there."

"Well don't look now but he's headed this way with Rhys."

Dominique's expression darkened, but she didn't turn around. "Sorry to do this, but I can't even be around him. If he was on fire I'd throw accelerant on him. I'll see you later." Just like that she was gone, hurrying in the other direction before Rhys and the apparent monster reached them.

The man frowned, his gaze following Dominique. "Who is your friend?" He had a slight Russian accent and was a freaking giant. The guy had to be at least six foot five and looked more like a thug with his shaved head and tattooed knuckles.

Raegan frowned at Rhys as he gave her a glass of champagne. She wasn't going to tell this stranger anything about her friend. Her date cleared his throat. "Ah, Viktor, this is Raegan. She works for Red Stone Security. I believe you have some acquaintances in common."

Blinking, the man turned back to look at her, as if seeing her for the first time, which obviously wasn't true since he'd asked her about Dominique.

"It's nice to meet you." He smiled politely, held out a hand that was surprisingly gentle when she took it.

"It's nice to meet you too." She turned to Rhys. "Will you give me a few minutes?" She didn't want to tell him in front of this stranger that she was concerned about Dominique so she motioned toward the back where the bathrooms were.

He smiled warmly. "Of course."

After ten minutes of searching she couldn't find Dominique anywhere. The event was pretty huge, but her friend stood out so Raegan wondered if she'd left. She'd already seen all three of her cousins, their wives, her uncle and his new fiancée, and Athena and her fiancé so it was a little off that she couldn't find Dominique. Unless...maybe she really was in one of the bathrooms.

She started to head to one of the closest ones when she saw a flash of yellow through the glass doors to the building connected to the event. The Celebration of Chefs was in an outdoor park-type area with lights and a gauzy canopy strung high in the air above them, creating a fairytale effect. It was nestled in between two buildings: an art center and a convention center. She knew from Athena that the catering company was using the facilities of the latter.

As she opened one of the glass doors a woman wearing black pants and a white button-down shirt—definitely one of the servers—smiled at her as she carried a tray of champagne flutes. "Would you like one?"

"Ah, no, but thanks." She'd already put down her drink earlier when searching and after last night she was feeling a little strange about drinking anything she hadn't seen poured. "Are there bathrooms back there?" She pointed in the direction she'd seen Dominique go. Because why else would Dominique be here?

"Yeah. You're not really supposed to use them, but other guests have been sneaking in. I won't tell." She winked conspiratorially before heading outside.

Raegan felt a little bad leaving Rhys, but she was worried about her friend. Dominique was one of the nicest people she'd met since moving to Miami and it was clear that man had upset her, even if he didn't seem to know who she was.

She passed a handful of caterers and partygoers as she headed across a big lobby. When she turned down the nearest hallway she spotted a woman in a pink and black cocktail dress coming out of the ladies room. She smiled at her before heading inside.

There were eight stalls including the handicapped one. She started at the end, gently pushing the doors open. Compared to outside it was freezing in here. A chill raked over her as she reached the fourth door. As she pushed it open, she heard the creaking of the main door opening right before the room was plunged into blackness.

"Someone's in here!" she called out. "Damn it." Blinking, she tried to adjust to the darkness but it was impossible. She took a step toward the door, but stopped as she heard a squeak.

Like a shoe against the tile.

A healthy dose of fear and paranoia slid through her veins. "Hello?"

When no one answered, she moved into the stall and locked the door. Stepping out of her heels, she picked one up to use as a weapon if need be. Maybe she was being paranoid but she didn't care. Not after last night.

With trembling hands, she pulled her phone from her clutch purse. Her heart hammered against her chest mercilessly as she heard another squeak. Then another.

Someone was definitely in here. And they'd turned the lights off intentionally.

"Think you can hide from me, whore?" a raspy male voice asked. It was like he was trying to hide his identity. Or maybe that was what he normally sounded like, but she didn't think so.

Pure panic punched through her as she stepped back. Her feet were cold against the floor and there was nowhere to go. She stepped up onto the seat of the toilet to give herself more distance as she covered her screen and dialed Grant. The phone started ringing as her fear skyrocketed.

"I've been watching you, know everything about you." The voice was closer now, somewhere outside the door. "You're a fucking tease." The door rattled once.

Oh, God. She held up her heeled shoe, prepared to use it as a weapon. It was the only thing she had. Damn it, she wished she'd thought to bring pepper spray, but her purse was small and she'd planned on being surrounded by people tonight.

Grant picked up on the second ring. "Hey, Raegan." His voice seemed loud in the enclosed space.

There was no way to hide what she was doing. "I'm trapped in the bathroom of the convention building with a man trying to hurt me! The first hallway off the right. I don't know if he's armed." The words fell out of her like machine gun fire. She wasn't sure how much time she'd have.

Grant cursed and she heard a crash, then, "I'm coming."

"You bitch!" The door rattled violently. "This isn't over," he snarled before the squeaks of his shoes hurried away.

She heard the door open but she wasn't sure if he'd truly left, could barely hear anything over the blood rushing in her ears.

Shaking, she stayed where she was, heel and phone in hand. She was aware of Grant saying something to her, but fear gripped her throat tight. She couldn't talk, couldn't do anything. And she hated herself for it. It was like fear rooted her in place.

Suddenly the lights were on, blinding her as the door slammed open. "Raegan!"

"I'm here." Oh God, he'd found her. As if she'd been released by an invisible string, she jumped down from the toilet and yanked the stall door open to find Grant racing toward her, his expression dark and a weapon in his hand.

She dropped her shoe as Porter, Harrison, her uncle and even Mara followed after him—all carrying guns like a civilian SWAT team. And she burst into tears.

* * *

Raegan knew she shouldn't be embarrassed. It wasn't as if any of this was her fault. But the level of humiliation she felt that the cops had been called to such a huge event, that all her cousins and their polished wives were witnessing all this, that her own date had been dragged away from the party because of this—it was embarrassing.

She felt like she'd ruined everyone's night, even if it wasn't her fault.

Someone had opened up a private room called 'Banquet Hall Two' at the center, and it was filled with her relatives, police and some other people she didn't know.

She sat at a round table drinking hot tea that Lizzy had brought her while Grant was talking to his former partner, Detective Carlito Duarte. Her own date had disappeared to get her a plate of food even though she'd told him not to bother. But it had seemed as if he wanted something to do after she'd subtly tried to brush off his concern. She knew he meant well but she didn't want him fussing over her. Thankfully Belle had gone with him as well.

And Lizzy was on the phone with her babysitter. Now her cousins and uncle were all huddled together by one of the exit doors, talking quietly, and they kept looking over at her. Even though it was the first time in the last hour that she'd been relatively alone, it made her feel like a bug under a microscope.

As she sat, Mara Caldwell, her cousin Harrison's wife, slid onto one of the cushioned chairs next to her, moving ghost quiet. Raegan was still a little stunned that Mara had burst in with the others earlier, a gun in her hand. And clearly she'd known how to handle it. She wasn't sure what Mara had done before moving to Miami but she guessed it was law enforcement.

"So, you look as if you want to run out of here," Mara said quietly.

She swallowed hard, wrapping her hands around the warm mug. "I'm really grateful everyone's here and the police responded so quickly."

Mara lightly squeezed Raegan's arm. "You still look overwhelmed. Tell me what to do and I'll do it for you."

The gesture from the normally hard-to-read woman made tears rush to the surface.

"Oh, hell, don't cry," Mara muttered, looking horrified.

Raegan sniffled, felt even more pathetic. "I can't help it," she muttered. "After last night and now this, I just want to go home and hide out for a week." Because what the hell was going on? Had she pissed off karma? First someone drugged her and now this?

Mara frowned, squeezed her hand once, before standing. "Sit tight."

Raegan watched in awe as Mara singlehandedly kicked almost everyone out of the room, including Uncle

Keith, until it was just Grant, Detective Duarte and Rae-gan. Well, and a uniformed officer by the door, but she was pretty sure he was there to keep people out. Mara gave her a thumbs up as she ushered the last person out of the room and left herself.

"Did they find anything on the security cameras?" she asked as the detective and Grant pulled up chairs and sat in front of her.

"There's nothing set up in this hallway—or most of them. Their security is focused around the exits more than anything. Cheaper for them," Carlito said, lifting a shoulder. But she saw the annoyance in his expression. He glanced once at Grant before looking back at her. "Have you been having any problems with anyone? A man who can't take no for an answer, who keeps asking you out? Anything unusual?"

She blinked, surprised by the questions. "No. I mean, yeah, I get asked out by men and sometimes I say no, sometimes yes. It's been a while since I've been on a date though. And I've never had any weirdos who kept asking once I said no."

"What about the man you're here with tonight?"

"Rhys? We're just friends."

Grant's mouth flattened, but he didn't say anything.

"You're sure he doesn't want more?" Carlito continued.

"I...I don't know but nothing's ever happened between us. Besides, didn't you," she looked at Grant, "say he was outside when I called you for help?"

Almost grudgingly, her cousin nodded. "Yeah."

"Tell me more about last night."

"Last night?" More surprise ricocheted through her, but it was hard not to make the connection of why he was asking. "You think the two things are linked?"

"I didn't say that. But I've got to be thorough—"

They all turned at the sound of raised voices.

She stood when Ford stormed in, looking a lot different than she'd ever seen him. He looked almost afraid, but totally in battle mode. Wearing cargo pants, a T-shirt and his weapon and badge, he looked ready to charge into a war zone. She wasn't sure why he was even there, but she didn't care. She was just relieved to see him.

She was moving before she'd fully processed the sight of him. He was faster than her, covering the distance across the largely empty banquet room in long strides.

"Are you okay?" he asked, his gaze roaming over her even as he pulled her into a close, very proprietary hug.

"I'm fine, I swear. Just shaken up." She held him back just as tightly, pressing her face against his chest. He felt good. Solid. She didn't want to let go but at the sound of a throat being cleared she stepped back to find Grant watching them.

Not with anger exactly, but his expression was as hard as his voice. "You didn't need to come down here. I just called you because you helped her last night."

So that was how he'd known. "Well 'her' is right here and I'm glad you called him." She turned in Ford's arms. "Grant's right though, you really didn't have to come—"

"Yeah, I did." Now he looked almost offended as he wrapped an arm around her shoulders.

Something that did not go unnoticed by Grant. She figured he'd want to have 'a talk' with her later but she was a grown woman and she really liked Ford. And she was grateful for his presence. Just having him here made everything seem bearable. She wrapped her arm around his waist and leaned into him, making her feelings clear to them all.

The detective cleared his throat. "I still need to finish interviewing Raegan. We can do it here or down at the station but I know she wants to get out of here."

Raegan guessed he was letting her make a statement here instead of taking her down to the police department because of his friendship and former partnership with Grant. "Here is fine with me."

Carlito nodded once before giving Grant an almost apologetic look. "I need you to wait in the hall with everyone else."

Next to her Ford tensed, as if waiting for the detective to say the same thing to him.

It was clear Grant wanted to argue, but after kissing her on the cheek and giving Ford a look of warning, he stalked out.

"I'm not going anywhere," Ford snapped.

Carlito just sighed. "I figured that. Come on. Let's sit down."

Once they were back at the table, Carlito cleared his throat. "Why didn't you report what happened last night?" Carlito asked Ford point-blank. "Grant filled me in on everything."

"Is this on the record?"

He sighed, leaned back in his chair. "Not if you don't want it to be."

"I don't. We both know how seriously her report would have been taken." He snorted at that, disgust in the sound. "There's nothing anyone could have done for her last night that I'm not already doing."

The detective raised an eyebrow. "What's that supposed to mean?"

"That tomorrow morning one of her cousins is meeting with the owner of the club she was at. He's bringing the security feeds. No warrant needed, no red tape. And you know what his reaction would have been if the cops had asked for the feeds. If possible, we'll get the identity of the guy who drugged her."

Well that was news to her. She shouldn't be surprised that none of her cousins had said anything, but she was annoyed Ford hadn't at least told her. Carlito's expression darkened and it was clear he didn't like that. She was sure there were a multitude of reasons he didn't.

The detective's jaw tightened once before he pushed out a sigh. "I get it, but I want you to make a report now," he said, focusing on her again. "I don't know that what happened tonight is connected to last night, but I don't believe in coincidence. I want this on the record so later, if this goes to court, there's a pattern of escalating behavior."

As his words sank in, chills spread through her like slow-moving ice. "You think...that's possible?" That the same person really wanted to hurt her enough to drug her then come after her so blatantly at a public venue a second time? She couldn't imagine anyone that angry at her. That this might end up in court someday made a wave of nausea sweep through her. "The guy in the bathroom, the things he called me...I don't know why."

"What did he call you?" Ford demanded.

"Ah, a whore and a tease." She winced as his expression darkened. The detective already knew, had put everything in his report.

Ford picked up one of her hands, linked his fingers through hers.

The detective gave her a hard look. "I think it's better to be prepared for the worst-case scenario."

"Okay, I'll make the report on that too. Do you mind if I tell my friend that he should just go ahead and leave?" Because she didn't want Rhys waiting around here any longer. It was unnecessary and she felt bad. For that matter, she was going to tell her cousins to leave too. Even if she knew it wouldn't do any good, she still had to try to get them out of here. There was no need to ruin everyone's night.

Ford's fingers tightened in hers slightly at the mention of her friend, but he didn't say anything otherwise. Just let her hand go when Carlito nodded that she could take a quick break.

When he stood, she shook her head. "My cousins are in the hall and so is my uncle. And all their significant others. I'll be fine, I promise." She actually wanted him with her, but she didn't want to throw it in Rhys's face that another man was taking her home, even if they were just friends. It felt mean somehow.

As she hurried across the room she felt Ford's heated stare on her back. As worried as she was right now, she

was still inordinately pleased that Ford had shown up tonight.

CHAPTER NINE

Tension knotted Ford's shoulders as he waited for Raegan to finish saying goodbye to Lizzy, Mara and Belle.

Keith, Harrison and Porter were all giving him what equaled death stares from across the room, but he didn't give a shit. They were pissed he was taking Raegan home—and probably that he was clearly interested in her—but they could get over it.

She brought out all his protective, possessive instincts and they could just deal with the fact that he was the one taking care of her. He would keep her safe.

Grant stepped back into the room and made a beeline for him. He'd been out in the hallway wrapping up with Duarte, a man Ford actually liked and had worked with on multiple occasions. He was a damn good detective, cared about finding justice and protecting the people of his city.

"So, you and my cousin?" Grant asked as he reached him, his voice low.

"I was going to tell you, and...we have our first date tomorrow night." He didn't know what else would happen, but he was into her. More into her than he could ever remember being with anyone. He knew he didn't want casual. Not even close. That little voice in his head still fucked with him, told him that she was too good to be true, but he ignored it.

Grant gave him a hard, assessing look. "We've all noticed the way you avoided looking at her at parties. And the way you'd sneak glances when you thought no one was paying attention. Which tells me all I need to know. So this isn't exactly a surprise, but..." He scrubbed a hand over his face. "Treat her right."

Or Grant—and likely his brothers—would kick his ass, was the implied threat.

That was a given. "I like her. A lot," he murmured, not wanting to say more. Guys didn't talk about shit like this and he wasn't going to start talking about his feelings now. It was time for a subject change. "Who's getting the security feeds, you or Porter?" He'd briefly talked to Grant about it when he'd called earlier but didn't know all the details.

"Ivanov is coming by tomorrow. He's personally picking up the recording from the offsite company the feeds go to. He's...not happy with his security team."

"Good." Though they both knew shit like this happened, even with the best security. From what Ford had seen, however, Viktor Ivanov needed to get a new team at his club. "Is he here tonight?"

"Yeah. Or he was earlier. I think he actually met Raegan but he probably doesn't know who she is."

"Is her friend gone?"

Grant's lips curved up. "Yeah. Can't believe you were okay with her coming here tonight with that fucker."

"She's a grown woman." He hadn't liked it, but it wasn't like he and Raegan were together. Not yet anyway.

But that was coming. "You think he's got anything to do with this?" For all Ford knew the guy didn't like being stuck in the friend zone. Maybe it was too much for him.

"Nah. And we ran the guy hard too."

Ford didn't doubt it, but nodded as Raegan broke away from her cousins-in-law and made her way to him and Grant. She looked beautiful and utterly exhausted.

"Can we go?" she sighed, moving to him like a magnet, wrapping her arm around his waist like it was the most natural thing in the world.

His slid his arm around her shoulders and pulled her close. He was glad she didn't want to hide their...relationship. Or whatever they had. That had been a fear, lurking in his subconscious. That she wouldn't want to let her cousins know about them. "If you're ready, we can leave."

"I'll follow you guys to your truck," Grant said, no room for argument in his voice.

Not that Ford planned to. He didn't care if Grant came along. More security was always better. He just cared about getting her home. Keeping her safe.

* * *

He wiped his damp palms against his pants as he steered into his garage. Tonight had been stupid.

He had been stupid.

What the hell had he been thinking?

He hadn't, that was the problem.

He'd seen Raegan in that hot-as-fuck dress and lost his mind. It was her fault for setting him off. She hadn't even noticed him. At work she always said hi and was friendly.

Way more friendly than she needed to be. But tonight she'd looked right through him, as if she had no idea who he was.

She'd been out with that guy he'd seen her with in the past. The rich one. After she'd been off with some other asshole this afternoon. Making out with that one like a whore for everyone to see.

From her texts and phone calls he didn't think she was fucking the one she'd been with tonight.

But he could be wrong.

God, he'd certainly been wrong tonight.

He was still shaking as he pressed the button to close his garage door. The trembles didn't stop when he was inside his house.

Shudders racked him.

He'd been careless, could have been caught. That was not on his agenda. Not like so many losers who 'wanted to get caught.' Fuck that.

He'd wanted to frighten her, to wrap his hand around her throat, to show her that he was in charge. He'd been so stupid though. Tonight had been too risky. Getting caught wasn't something he ever wanted. It was why he didn't send her threatening messages, contact her. It would leave a way to be traced back to him. Instead, he just watched. Waiting for the right time. He did actually write her letters, he just never sent them. Once he had her in his possession, he'd let her read them then.

She was his secret obsession. He loved watching, but he was tired of women teasing him, tired of being invisible.

He ran a hand over his erection as he shut the mud-room door behind him. He shouldn't even want her, but he couldn't help it. She called to him.

He still wondered if he'd worked her up in his mind, made her out to be something she wasn't. When he'd first met her he'd thought she was sweet, innocent. Now she seemed like every other woman. Just another whore.

He didn't bother changing, just went straight into his workout room and slammed his fist against his punching bag.

The impact against his knuckles loosened some of the rage building inside him, let him focus and channel his energy.

He had to get back under control. After his slipup to-night, he had to be back in command. He'd likely see her next week, get his temporary fix. He'd only gone to the event tonight to see her. After reading her texts he'd known she'd be there. One look at her was all he'd wanted. When she'd separated herself from her date, the opportunity to scare her had been too much. If she hadn't had her stupid phone—something he would have thought of if he'd been thinking clearly—he'd have been able to do more than scare her. He could have touched her, shown her that she was his.

He slammed his fist into the punching bag again and again, imagined pummeling the man she'd been with to-night. Or the other one from the beach. Both. It didn't matter.

They were both obstacles.

Maybe... Maybe Raegan wanted him to fight for her, to show her that he could eliminate any competition.

That he was the right man for her. Women liked that shit, when guys were all alpha.

His arms were sore and sweat was pouring down his face and neck by the time he forced himself to stop punching the bag.

He was finally back under control, his head clear. And he wouldn't be making a mistake like tonight again. He was done waiting and writing letters he never sent. Next time he went after her, he was taking her. Simple as that.

CHAPTER TEN

Raegan wanted to tell Ford that he didn't need to
check her condo, not since she'd had her security
system armed. But it would have been a fruitless effort.
He was totally geared up, the energy rolling off him a little
intense.

He'd point-blank told her uncle that he'd be the one
taking her home and looking after her. And nobody ever
told Keith Caldwell anything.

She certainly hadn't disagreed, even if she didn't need
someone to look after her. Not in her own home.

Tonight had scared the hell out of her but she felt safe
in her home. And while she didn't necessarily feel like an
obligation to him, she also didn't want this to be a defin-
ing thing in their potential relationship.

He was older than her and likely way more experienced. She liked that. But she also didn't want him to feel
like she needed taking care of. It made things feel too un-
equal between them.

While he did a full-scale sweep of her place, she
headed to the kitchen and pulled out a bottle of Tylenol.
She took two with a glass of red wine instead of water
because yeah, it was one of those nights.

"Ugh," she muttered to herself, hating the whole situation.

"What's wrong?" Ford was suddenly there in her small kitchen, his expression worried.

Half smiling, she shook her head. "Nothing. Just annoyed in general." Even thinking that the person who'd tried to attack her tonight was the same one from last night was beyond scary. She always thought stalkers left creepy messages and made heavy breathing phone calls. If someone had been harassing her, she'd have gone to the police. And her cousins. It was like this insanity had come out of the blue.

"Do you want to rest?" Ford looked unsure what to do as he stood there. As if he wished he had a specific target to fight.

"No. Look, thank you for driving me home and for coming to the event when Grant called you. That was so sweet. But don't feel like you need to stay or anything. Or to take care of me." She wanted that out there, wanted him to understand she didn't want to be—

"Oh, I'm staying."

She blinked at his matter-of-fact tone. "Excuse me?"

"On the couch, but I'm staying. Or I'll walk you up to Porter and Lizzy's place. You're not going to be alone tonight."

His bossy tone rankled her. Setting her wine glass down, she pushed away from the counter and stalked toward him. "I'm grateful for what you've done, but you don't get to tell me what to do."

"Pretty sure I just did," he answered, his gaze dropping to her mouth.

She was torn between being offended and turned on. Raegan didn't like men to tell her what to do. She didn't

like *anyone* to tell her what to do. 'A problem with au-
thority,' her mother had always said.

But heat pooled between her thighs at that take-
charge tone of Ford's. She certainly wasn't going to tell
him that—it would just encourage him. She placed a hand
on his chest. "Ford—"

He covered her hand with his bigger, callused one and
lifted it. Taking her completely by surprise, he skated his
lips over her knuckles. As he did, he let out a shuddering
breath. "When I got that call I was terrified for you."

Immediately she softened, stepping even closer to
him. He was such a solid presence. "I'm okay."

"I'm still staying over." Once again his tone was all
domineering.

"You can't do that," she muttered.

"Do what?" He stepped closer, moving until he had her
back against the counter and there was nowhere for her
to go.

Even as his bossiness annoyed her, she wanted to arch
into him, to rub up against him like a feline in heat. Everything about the man was sexy, and this need he seemed
to have to take charge was insanely hot even if it was
maddening. Clearly she should have her head examined.
This type of behavior had never turned her on before.
Once a guy tried to tell her what to do, she was out the
door. Now, however… "Drive me crazy being all caveman."

"I think you like it." There was a hint of a question in
his statement. His green eyes seemed darker tonight, as
he looked down at her with blatant heat and hunger.

"You would think that." Even if it was true she wasn't going to tell him.

"If I slid my hand up your dress and cupped that pretty pussy, would I find you wet?" His voice was raspy, unsteady and there was no mistaking he was turned on, given his thick erection pressing against her.

Her mouth fell open at his words. She'd never had a man talk to her like that. The rawness, the dirtiness of the words got her even wetter. She swallowed hard. "Why don't you find out?"

He blinked once, as if she'd surprised him, but just as quickly, he moved into action. One hand slid behind her, gripped the counter tight as he leaned into her.

The only sound was their breathing, and that seemed over-pronounced as his other hand reached between them and slowly began pushing her cocktail dress up. The rustling of her dress seemed just as loud as their breathing. She was surprised she could hear anything anyway with her heart beating in her ears.

Nerves danced in her belly when his fingers grazed her inner thighs, barely touching her. Another rush of heat pooled between her legs at the teasing.

He had her pinned in place with his gaze when he slid her panties to the side, stroked a finger through her slick folds.

"This for me, baby?" he murmured, his eyes still trained on her mouth.

Her nipples tightened at the feel of him touching her so intimately. "Yes," she whispered, loving how he called her baby or sweetheart. Oh, how she wanted him to push inside her. Her inner walls clenched, needing to be filled, but he just slowly stroked against her folds, barely penetrating her.

She rolled her hips against his hand and he shuddered. "You're killing my good intentions."

She clutched onto his shoulders, needing him for support. "What intentions?" she rasped out.

"You need rest," he murmured, even as he slid a finger over her clit, gently massaging.

No, what she needed was more of this. But she couldn't find her voice when he increased the pressure.

She started to close her eyes when his lips covered hers. Unlike their kiss at the beach, this one was slow, sensual, as if he didn't mind taking his time. The pacing was just as easy as his gentle strokes against her clit.

She had no idea what Ford wanted, or whether this was just casual for him.

He nipped her bottom lip. "I want to taste you." His words came out guttural.

She moaned into his mouth, pretty much the only response she was capable of when he was touching her so intimately. But he was already tasting her— *Oh.* It took a few seconds for her brain to catch up to his meaning. She felt her cheeks flush as he grasped the edge of her panties and tugged them down.

Gravity did its job and when they reached her ankles she stepped out of them.

"I want to taste your come, to feel you climaxing against my mouth." He lifted her onto the counter and she couldn't find any words as he kneeled between her legs.

The sight of his dark head between her spread thighs under the bright light of her kitchen was one of the most erotic things she'd ever seen.

He looked even bigger like that, his shoulders broader than she'd realized. And talk about exposed. She'd never felt so vulnerable and turned on before.

It was clear that Ford had a lot of experience and liked talking dirty. She'd never been a big talker during sex and wondered if he wanted that. She wasn't going to start now because she figured anything she said would sound stupid.

He didn't seem to mind her quietness though. Not when he inhaled deeply before burying his face between her legs.

And that's when she lost the ability to talk or really think about anything other than the pleasure he was giving her.

He swiped his tongue up the length of her folds, practically growling against her. She felt the subtle vibration trickle out to her nerve endings. And the way his facial hair teased her inner thighs made her just as crazy.

Sliding her fingers through his short hair, she held on for dear life.

"Feet on my shoulders, spread wider," he demanded against her body.

She did what he said, feeling even more exposed. He shoved his tongue deeper inside her after she shifted position.

"Ford," she groaned, shudders racking her as he continued teasing her with his wicked, talented tongue. His beard rubbed against her folds now too, not just her inner thighs. The sensation was different...stimulating.

When he reached up and began massaging her clit with his thumb at the same time, she lost it. She hadn't even realized how close she was to climax, but the pressure was intense, perfect.

"Right there. Don't stop. Please." The last word came out as a plea, but she didn't care. She *didn't* want him to stop.

He increased the pressure against her sensitive bundle of nerves even as he increased the stroke of his tongue. It was all too much.

Her orgasm slammed into her, sending a shock of pleasure out to all her nerve endings in a harsh, pulsing wave that had all her muscles tightening. Oh God, it had been so long since she'd felt anything remotely close to this. And her vibrator had nothing on Ford's talented tongue.

She was a quivering mass of nerves when Ford finally stopped, the teasing too much for her sensitive flesh.

When he stood, the hunger in his gaze was scorching as he watched her. And when he crushed his mouth to hers, the only thing she knew was that she needed him inside her right now.

He said something against her mouth, but she couldn't make it out. Something about her taste. Buzzing with adrenaline, she reached between their bodies, grasped at his belt buckle and pants even as she felt him unzip the back of her dress. Next he stripped off his shirt.

The material of her dress slid to her waist, cool air rushing over her already hard nipples as she shoved his pants down.

His tongue teased hers as he slid a finger inside her, and groaned again. Scooting to the edge of the counter, she grasped his cock, stroked once. Twice.

He pulled back, his neck muscles corded tight as he seemed to struggle to breathe. "Fuck, Raegan."

Feeling insanely powerful, she stroked him again, watched the way his whole body reacted. He rolled his hips once into her hold, but just as quickly he moved her hand aside and positioned himself between her thighs. Apparently he liked to be in control.

She stared down at his thick length and grew even wetter. The man was big all over. Feeling it and seeing it were two different things. She rolled her hips against him as he thrust inside her.

He cupped the back of her head and held firm as he buried himself deep. "You're so fucking tight." His words were harsh.

She couldn't talk at all, and couldn't believe he could. Not when he felt so damn good inside her. As he began thrusting, she let her head fall back and closed her eyes. Pleasure rolled through her with each push inside her.

He kissed a path up her neck, nibbling at her earlobe as he continued those long, steady strokes. She arched into him, sliding her hands up his broad chest, digging her fingers into him as her inner walls started to tighten quicker and quicker around him. She hadn't thought she'd be able to come again, but her body said otherwise.

When his head dipped suddenly and he sucked on one of her nipples, her eyes flew open and she jerked from the sharp pleasure pervading her body once again. As a second orgasm crested inside her, he groaned against her breast, his whole body trembling.

He drew back as his thrusts grew faster, wilder, until all his muscles pulled taut. The lines and striations in his arms were more defined as he emptied himself inside her, his shout of pleasure raw and harsh.

As his thrusts slowed and he grew soft inside her, she buried her face against his chest, inhaled his scent. She loved the way he smelled, a spicy musk.

His big hands settled on her hips, his breathing steadying as his chin rested on her head. Suddenly he stiffened and muttered a short curse.

She couldn't imagine what was wrong until he said the word, "Condom."

That was when she realized they hadn't used one. *Crap, crap, crap.* It had been so long since she'd been with anyone that she hadn't thought about it. Okay, the truth was, she hadn't been thinking, period. Which wasn't a good excuse, just the way it was.

Cringing, she pulled back to look up at him. "I'm on the pill." She had been since she was fifteen, thanks to an erratic menstrual cycle and horrible cramps.

He let out a sigh of relief and she didn't blame him. She wanted kids—eventually. But not anytime soon.

"I'm sorry, Raegan. That was fucked up of me. I should have—"

"There are two of us right here. I forgot too. God, I wasn't even thinking." She didn't like him shouldering all the blame.

He shook his head, his expression annoyed, clearly at himself. "I've never had sex without a condom. And I'm clean. I was tested six months ago and it's been about a year since I've been with anyone. I'll get tested again though if you want."

"I haven't been with anyone since..." Ugh, she didn't want to say it out loud. But she couldn't hold back, not when he was being honest, not when they were talking about something serious. And not when she was wet with his come between her thighs. "Since my college boyfriend. Almost three years ago," she rushed out, just wanting to get it out of the way. "I'm clean."

He looked surprised, maybe at how long it had been for her, then he simply crushed his mouth over hers with one of those sexy growls she felt all the way to her toes. She wrapped her legs around his waist as he lifted her off the counter. He was already growing hard again, which was a big surprise, but a welcome one.

She lost her dress completely and he lost the rest of his pants on the way to her...living room. Yeah, they weren't making it to the bed tonight. Not this second time anyway. Her back hit the couch and then they toppled to the floor.

He lifted up on his arms so he wouldn't squish her, caging her in beneath him. He let out a short laugh. "Shit, sorry."

"Don't be." She grinned, happier than she'd been in a long time. Even with all the insanity of the last couple days, she was still glad that it had inadvertently brought her and Ford together.

She just hoped that this meant something more to him too. That this wasn't a one-time thing. He'd seemed okay with her going to the event tonight with another man, even if she had told him that they were friends. Her own cousins had been annoyed with her—because they apparently didn't want her to even talk to the opposite sex—but not Ford. She should be glad he hadn't been all stupid caveman about that, but still, she wished she knew if he did care. If this was more than just physical for him. She wouldn't focus on that now, didn't want to bring herself down from the high of being with him.

In the morning she'd deal with reality.

* * *

Ford frowned at the sound of Raegan's front doorbell going off. She was in the shower and it was too damn early for anyone to be here. Anyone other than her relatives. Which didn't create a problem, but he didn't like throwing it in Grant's face that he was sleeping with Raegan.

Sighing, he pulled on his clothes from yesterday, sans his work belt, but he still kept his weapon in hand. Right now he wasn't going to let his guard down when it came to Raegan.

After looking through the peephole he grimaced. It was Grant and Porter. Tucking his pistol away, he disarmed her security system and opened the door.

Both men stared at him, Porter more in surprise than Grant. Just as quickly that surprise turned to annoyance and something a little more heated. Ford didn't have a sister, and it was clear the Caldwell brothers thought of Raegan more like a sister than a cousin, so he could understand their annoyance at finding him here.

"Look, before we go any further," he said, not bothering to ask them why they were on Raegan's doorstep at seven in the morning, "you need to know that this isn't casual for me." He kept his focus on Porter since he was the one who seemed annoyed about it and he'd already told Grant this. "I like Raegan a lot and unless she tells me otherwise, I'm not going anywhere."

Porter seemed to relax at his words, and gave a sharp nod. "Good. You hurt her, I hurt you." He said it so matter-of-fact, not waiting for a response as he continued. "We got the security feed from the convention center. The cops are still waiting on a warrant to get a copy, but my dad called in a favor."

Ford stepped back and let them in as Porter pulled out a USB drive. "Got a ton of footage on here and for all we know, there's nothing useful. We just thought Raegan might recognize someone from last night and be able to place him at the club too. Which is nothing the cops can use unless she can pick out the guy who tried to take her Friday."

"She says her memory's a blank from that night," Ford muttered. Fucking GHB did that to people, wiped out blocks of time. And he hadn't gotten a good-enough look at the guy that night, not with that fucking hoodie and sunglasses, to give a description or even pick someone out of a lineup.

"I know. Still, if she recognizes someone not even from Friday but somewhere else, someone she's seen around and didn't realize until now, maybe it'll trigger something in her memory and hopefully we'll be able to narrow down who's after her."

"So you think the two nights are related?" He'd had a bad feeling about that.

Both Grant and Porter shrugged and Porter said, "We're not ruling anything out."

"Good." Because he wasn't either. It just seemed like too much coincidence that she'd been drugged, some guy had tried to take her out of the club and then someone had come after her when she was alone last night.

If last night hadn't happened he would have written off Friday night as bad fucking luck. Now...he was going to be on guard 24/7 until they caught this asshole.

CHAPTER ELEVEN

When he looked into Raegan's office, his breathing automatically grew ragged, his heart rate ratcheting up. She wasn't here—probably in a meeting because it was too early for lunch—but this was her space. It even smelled like her. When he started to get aroused, he stepped away from her office door.

Glancing down the hallway, he saw that there was a normal amount of activity on this floor. Plenty of armed men and women going about their business. Raegan wasn't armed of course, but he'd never be stupid enough to try to take her or hurt her in the Red Stone building. He'd never get out alive.

But he liked being around her things, liked imagining her touching her things, talking on the phone.

Since he had no business being in her and her boss's office, he continued down the hallway. It wouldn't do to get caught being inside her space. He'd be able to talk his way out of it if he was caught, he had no doubt. He could just pretend he'd gotten mixed up with office numbers.

But if he did that, someone might remember he'd been somewhere he wasn't supposed to be. Then later, once he had Raegan, someone could remember and report it to her family. It wasn't the police he was worried about, but the Caldwell family.

He didn't know much about Keith Caldwell, but he'd heard the rumors that he was a dangerous man. No, he wouldn't risk getting on anyone's radar. After he took Raegan, he wouldn't even change up his routine. At least not for a month or so.

He had it all planned out. Once he got her to his place, she'd be his. He had a room specifically set up for her. It had plenty of insulation so no one would be able to hear her scream. Not that he wanted to hurt her. He just wanted her to be his. Once he convinced her they were meant to be together everything would be okay.

Just taking her was the biggest problem. She was always surrounded by people. Pushing his cart down the hall, he smiled and nodded at people he saw almost every day.

Keeping up his façade was becoming more difficult, but for Raegan he could do it. To have her, he could do anything.

* * *

Ford loved his job, especially now that he was at the range full time training officers. He'd briefly been on patrol, had done undercover work and been part of the drug task force for a while in addition to being part of SWAT, but the training was where he really excelled.

It had surprised him, but not his superiors when they'd promoted him. He'd thought he would miss being on the streets, but this was a different kind of fulfilling.

Except today, when all he wanted to do was get the hell out of here. He'd been looking at his watch every ten minutes, practically counting down until he could leave. Because all he wanted to do was see Raegan. She'd asked him if he wanted to come over tonight and he planned to cook for her.

At least to start the night. Then he planned to have her naked and under him for hours.

Stopping in front of his locker, he rolled his shoulders as he slid off his shoulder holster. Today had been long and tiring, and right about now he wanted a hot shower and Raegan on a platter. As he started to strip off his T-shirt his phone buzzed in his pocket. He always kept it on silent out at the range, and sometimes he didn't bring it at all.

Today he'd wanted to be available if Raegan needed him. When he saw her name on his caller ID his heart rate jacked up triple time. He couldn't remember the last time a woman had gotten him this worked up.

Try never.

"Hey," he said, answering on the second buzz.

"Hey yourself."

He smiled at the sound of her voice, pressure easing inside his chest. Even though he knew her cousins had had an undercover guard with her all day, hearing her on the other end of the phone made him feel sane again. "How was work?"

"Long, tiring," she said, laughter in her voice. "And unfortunately I'm not done." Now there was regret.

Disappointment swelled inside him as he realized she was going to cancel their plans, but he understood she had to work. He leaned one shoulder against the neighboring locker. The room was mostly empty, almost everyone except another trainer gone for the day. "You have to stay late?"

"Yeah. It's... I'll fill you in later. I still want to do dinner tonight though, if you're game?"

"Yes." He didn't care what time, he just wanted to see her, to hold her in his arms again. He loved the way she blushed so very prettily when he talked dirty. Every time they'd been naked together over the weekend, she'd seemed to get even wetter the more he said, which had taken him by surprise. "What time were you thinking?"

"Seven thirty, eight, which I know is kinda late for dinner. If you want to cancel, I understand."

He snorted. "I'll be there. Still want me to cook?"

"That sounds like heaven." He could hear the fatigue in her voice, wished he was there to hold her.

Yesterday she'd looked over the feeds her cousins had brought over, to the point of exhaustion. Unfortunately she hadn't seen anyone she recognized leaving the conference center. "Did Porter get those other security feeds today?" The owner of the club was supposed to have brought them over.

"Yeah. He texted me about it, but I've got too much to do. I'd planned to look at them on my lunch break but Athena and I ended up having a work meeting I didn't want to miss."

"I'm sure Athena wouldn't mind if you skipped one." Especially for something like this.

"I know, but..." She trailed off, sighing. "I know it's stupid, but I almost don't want to see the video. I don't want to see myself when I can't remember most of that night. It's scary." She whispered the last part.

He wanted to pummel whoever had drugged her—and likely gone after her at the event Saturday—right then and there. "Want me to watch it with you tonight?"

"If you don't mind."

There was a hint of hesitation in her voice that surprised him. "Of course I don't."

"Then yeah, I'd really appreciate it. Listen…I'm not going to be dating anyone else. I don't even know what we are or where we're headed, and I know we're just starting whatever this thing is. But I've never dated more than one guy at a time. Okay, that's not true. I tried but it's just not me." The words came out in a rush, as if she'd been practicing. "Considering we had sex this weekend, a lot of sex, without a condom, I'd appreciate it if you'd tell me if you—"

He shoved up from the locker. "Raegan, I'm not dating anyone else and I don't plan to. I don't want anyone else but you." Which he probably shouldn't admit either, but fuck it. He'd never been one to play relationship games. He wanted her to know where they stood, and while he wouldn't push her for exclusivity or a commitment—yet—he liked knowing she wouldn't be dating anyone else right now.

She let out a short breath of air. "Okay, then."

He bit back a laugh at the way she said it, as if she'd been expecting a different response or something. "So I'll see you tonight?"

"Yes. I've already let security know to expect you so they'll buzz you up whenever you get there."

"Good. Listen, you, uh..." He knew he didn't have a right to ask, but he couldn't help but be worried about her. "You gonna have a guard with you the rest of the evening?"

She snorted softly. "Grant told you about that?"

"Yeah."

"Why am I not surprised? And yes, his name's Travis. He's been a shadow to both me and Athena all day. He's coming with me this evening as well."

"Good." That eased most of the tension in his chest, but until he was with her, nothing would completely do that. "See you soon."

After they disconnected he realized he was grinning like a fool. He probably looked like a jackass but he didn't care. Raegan, one of the sweetest—and yeah, sexiest—women he'd ever known, would be crying out his name later tonight as he made her come against his mouth. She'd been so damn sexy Saturday night, coming apart against him like that the first time.

"I recognize that look," Kip Rawlings, another trainer, muttered as he stepped up to his own locker and yanked it open.

Ford pulled his bag out of his locker, ignoring his normally laid-back friend. The past couple weeks Kip had been a giant asshole and nothing was going to ruin Ford's mood today.

"You seeing someone?" Kip asked as he started stripping.

Ford sat on the long bench, took off his boots. "Yeah." He wasn't going to give more details than that. Normally he would have, but fuck. Whatever had crawled up Kip's ass had made the guy piss on everything lately.

Kip muttered something about women being bitches as he sat on the bench next to him.

Ford couldn't rein it in anymore. "Dude, what the fuck is your problem lately?"

Kip let his shoes drop but didn't turn to look at Ford. Just sat there staring at his locker. "Robin's leaving me. She's been cheating on me for months. I found out, confronted her and she didn't deny it. Said she's been unhappy for a long time. That she's just glad we didn't have kids together because it can be a clean break between us. Easy for everyone," he muttered, bitterness lacing each word. "Easy for her, maybe."

Oh, hell. Ford had never liked Robin, but that wasn't the kind of thing you said to a friend. And he'd been there, understood what the guy was going through. "Sorry, man."

His friend lifted a shoulder.

"That why you've been such a dick the last couple weeks?"

Kip snorted and half laughed, which was what Ford had been going for. "Sorry, man. Yeah." He scrubbed a hand over his face. "I'm not handling it well. Clearly."

"I've been there." And it had been a dark time in his life. "Want to grab a couple drinks?"

Kip finally looked at him, dark circles under his eyes. "Yeah. Maybe dinner too? I don't want to go home, man."

Ford nodded. He had time before Raegan was off work. "Of course. Let me grab a shower and we'll head out."

Kip nodded and didn't make a move from his seat so Ford grabbed his bag and headed for the showers.

Turned out it was a good thing Raegan had to work late. He hated that his friend was going through this, but Robin had never been a good partner in Ford's opinion anyway. Not that he was going to say any of that to his friend. And not that he was much of an expert anyway.

Nah, he'd just take Kip out, let him blow off some steam and probably be the designated driver if Kip wanted to put back a few. After Ford's ex had cheated on him things had been crappy for a while. He'd never imagined wanting to get serious with anyone again. Until Raegan. Deep down he hated that he worried the same thing would happen with her. He didn't like being that guy, worried the woman he was with would cheat.

* * *

"So who's this mystery woman you're dating?" Kip leaned back in his seat, seeming more relaxed than he'd been in weeks. He brought his bottled beer to his mouth, took a long drag.

Ford shrugged. He didn't want to talk about Raegan. He knew it was bullshit, but cops were superstitious as a rule. He didn't want to jinx what had just started to develop between them. Plus he didn't want to rub it in Kip's face, regardless. "Just someone I met."

Kip snorted and waved their server over. "That's an evasive answer if I ever heard one." As the woman approached he ordered another basket of wings and a beer for him.

Ford had decided to make it a one-beer night and it looked like he'd be driving Kip home anyway. They'd chosen a local hangout on Bayside that had good beer, cheap eats and a bunch of big screen televisions with various games on. "You got a lawyer yet, or what?"

"I've talked to a few. I keep hoping she'll change her mind."

Which meant he was waiting for Robin to make the first move. Ford wanted to tell him he should make a move and take control now, but knew that wasn't what his friend wanted to hear. He just hated that Kip was holding out hope. "I can give you my brother's info if you want. He doesn't do divorces but he'll know someone good."

Kip nodded, glanced at the TV above the bar. They were at a booth next to a huge window that overlooked the street and half a dozen shops. Ford didn't like feeling so exposed, but he liked having a visual of the street.

"Wait, your brother?" Kip seemed to jerk to life as he turned back to face him. "Fuck that guy."

Ford gave him a wry smile. Kip knew about everything that had gone down between them. "It's water under the bridge." Even if it *wasn't*, Dallas was still a damn good attorney. "He'll be able to give you a good recommendation. It's better than going into this blind."

"Yeah, maybe." He frowned though, clearly not liking the idea. "I'll be back in a sec. Gotta hit the head."

Ford nodded, turning to look out the window, scanning the people out of habit. He was always looking for a threat, it seemed. Unfortunately this had been the only free booth when they'd arrived. For a Monday night it was pretty busy, but people were getting off work and this place was close to one of the hospitals, the police department and even Red Stone. He'd almost texted Raegan to let her know he'd be nearby in case she got finished with her work thing early, but he didn't want to bug her.

After getting burned badly before, he could admit he was gun-shy when it came to relationships. Raegan had him letting his guard down though. Everything about her seemed real, sweet and honest. Still...he kept waiting for the shit to hit the fan, to find out she wasn't as perfect as he'd made her out to be.

He laughed to himself when he saw her get out of an SUV across the street. Shouldn't be a surprise, not when her work was so close. A man he vaguely recognized, wearing a dark suit, got out after her.

Ford could immediately tell the guy had training as he scanned the surrounding area, his posture stiff, alert. Just watching her, his heart rate increased.

Her long dark hair was down in soft waves and she had on a vivid blue wraparound dress with heels. She was too far away for him to truly appreciate her, but the way the dress hugged her body had him primed to peel it from her later tonight. He'd tell her to leave the shoes on as he went down on her. Seven thirty couldn't come soon enough.

When her 'friend' from Saturday night got out of the vehicle next, his good mood darkened. The guy set his hand on the small of Raegan's back as they stepped up onto the sidewalk, his body language completely territorial.

"Just friends, my ass," he muttered. Even if Raegan thought so, clearly her 'friend' didn't. Ford had only gotten a glance at him the other night and he didn't like him. He wanted more than friendship with Raegan. And what the hell was he doing with her anyway? She'd said she had a work thing.

Feeling like he was spying, Ford started to look away when the guy leaned in and kissed her on the mouth. The sight was like a punch to Ford's gut. He stared for what felt like forever until Kip's voice jerked his attention away.

"They haven't brought the wings out yet? I'm freaking starving," his friend muttered, sliding into the booth across from him.

Just like that his surroundings came back into focus again. The laughter of patrons, some people shouting at the TVs, the general buzz of energy in the place. It all rushed back, rolling over him even as iciness invaded his veins.

He tried to tell himself it was a misunderstanding, but...what the fuck. And she'd said she had a work thing. That did *not* look like work.

Their relationship might be new, but after earlier he believed her when she said she wouldn't be seeing anyone else. Or he had believed her. He should have learned his lesson before.

He rolled his shoulders once, and against his better judgment looked out the window again. He couldn't see any of them anymore, just the big SUV they'd arrived in. Which was just as well. He didn't need another visual of Raegan with that asshole.

He wanted to give her the benefit of the doubt but the past punched its way to the surface, that little voice in his head telling him that of course she was too good to be true. That guy was wealthy and had everything to offer her. God, he was such an idiot.

CHAPTER TWELVE

Raegan shoved at Rhys's chest, her heart racing, but not in a good way, as he stepped back. "What the hell was that?" Her palm itched to smack him right across the face.

To give him credit, he looked like he felt awful. "I...read your signals wrong. Really wrong," he muttered. "I'm sorry."

"Guys, either move back into the SUV or let's head inside." Travis Sanchez, a man from the office—and a friend—had been her official shadow today. Right now he looked a little like he wanted to deck Rhys, though he was curbing his impulse. He'd been with her when she'd been in Vegas and in the aftermath of the kidnapping and had been a little overly protective since. This was a man she trusted and genuinely liked.

She glanced up and down the sidewalk, annoyed that this jackass had kissed her without her permission, and embarrassed that Travis had seen it all. People were walking by in twos and threes, some talking on their cell phones and some carrying way too many shopping bags. No one was paying any attention to them at all, but he was right. "We'll get in the SUV. I'm sorry—"

"Don't be sorry, Raegan," Travis murmured, holding the door open. "I'll give you a couple minutes alone but I'm right here if you need me." He patted his jacket pocket too and she realized he was making sure he still had the vehicle keys. Probably so Rhys couldn't run off with her. Not that she was actually worried about *that*, but she'd come to realize that the security personnel of Red Stone didn't think like civilians. To them, anyone was a threat.

She slid into the back seat of the SUV, moving over so Rhys could follow suit.

"I'm very sorry, Raegan. I thought...well, it doesn't matter what I thought."

Part of her wanted to let it go. The 'polite' girl she'd been taught to be would have let this go a couple years ago. But after moving to Miami, after being freaking kidnapped, she'd learned a lot about herself in the last year. "You're right. It doesn't matter what you thought. I told you we could be friends and I thought you were okay with that. I've never given you any indication I wanted more. If you thought you read my signals wrong, I don't know what signals you're talking about. *You* contacted Red Stone today, wanting to work with us on an event. And I know that you requested you work with me. Athena told me. I haven't been pursuing you or sending any fucking signals." She snapped out the last part, taking both of them off guard.

She rarely cursed and especially not in work mode. But after Friday and Saturday night she was feeling more than out of sorts and she was shaking with anger the longer she thought about the way he'd just kissed her without her permission. It was making her second-guess herself. Maybe she'd been 'too' friendly with him before, but...she didn't think so. And it didn't matter if she had been friendly. That was part of her damn job and, you know, just being a decent person. She shouldn't have to worry about some guy kissing her because he thought she'd given some imaginary signal.

"You're right. I'm incredibly sorry." His accent was thicker now, the distress punching off him seemingly sincere. "I've...never had to chase after a woman. Ever. We've been spending time together and I obviously read things wrong. I'm embarrassed by the way I've acted. There's no excuse for what I did."

She softened a little, but not much. Nodding stiffly, she said, "Apology accepted, but I won't be working with you on this project. You can work with Athena or someone else." They'd hired two more full-time staff in the last five months in the event coordination department, so he could take his pick.

He looked as if he wanted to protest, but nodded. "Of course."

Awkwardness settled in the interior until Travis opened the driver's seat door. He slid behind the wheel, and looked at Raegan, not Rhys, something she really appreciated. "We staying or going, Raegan?"

"Let's head back to the office." She was pretty much at her limit for yearly bullshit and it was only the summer. Right now she wanted to put as much distance between her and Mr. Jackass sitting next to her.

She needed to tell Athena, of course. And unfortunately she'd have to tell Porter, otherwise he'd find out and just get annoyed with her for keeping him in the dark. And he was her first choice to tell because he had the most level head of all her cousins and uncle. She simply didn't want to deal with anything else right now. It was like karma had decided to crap on her this week.

At least she'd get to see Ford soon. At that thought, she looked out the window and smiled to herself. Despite the insanity of the last few days, Ford was the silver lining in everything.

* * *

Once she was safe and alone in her condo, Raegan slipped off her high heels and stripped off her clothes as she made her way to her bedroom. She had enough time for a hot shower before Ford got here and she needed it. Though the idea of inviting him in to join her was more than appealing, she needed some downtime to herself.

When she heard her phone ding in her purse, she practically scrambled for it, hopeful that it was Ford telling her he was on his way. She saw his name on the screen before she swiped her code in.

Got caught up, won't be able to make it tonight. Sorry.

She blinked at the shortness of his text. It was abrupt and unlike him, but it was hard to read tone in a text. Still, she frowned. *You can still come over*, she typed back. *I don't care how late.*

There was a pause, then, *Don't think I'll be able to.*

She fought the disappointment that swelled inside her, but it was a fruitless effort. Her fingers swiped across the screen. *How about you cook for me tomorrow, then? I want to see if you're as good as you say.*

A longer pause this time before, *Not sure what my schedule looks like. I'll let you know.*

Oooookay. She sat on the edge of her bed, not sure what to make of this conversation at all. Heck, she wasn't even sure how to respond so she went with something generic. *Hope you have a good rest of the night, talk to you later.*

His response was just as generic and depressing. *Sure.*

Tossing her phone onto the bed, she headed for her shower. "Screw you, Monday," she muttered to herself.

* * *

"Would you mind grabbing takeout for us at the restaurant?" Jules asked Ruby as she stepped out from the back storeroom. "I've already called up there but I want to unload a couple of the new shipments."

Ruby glanced up from the cash register where she was running reports. They would be closing in about fifteen minutes and her aching feet were grateful. "Sure, no problem. Want me to lock the door on the way out?"

"Yeah, since I'll be in the storeroom."

"Sweet. I'll grab the food and be back in a bit." They had a ton of new shipments in and she knew Jules wanted to unload at least half of them tonight so they could start stocking tomorrow. As soon as she was back with the food, she was taking off her heels and slipping into her comfy slippers.

The walk to Julieta's parents' restaurant was short, only a block away. The street was quiet tonight, with most of the shoppers long gone or already settled in at one of the restaurants in the area. In an older, established residential Miami neighborhood, their street was the only one with shops and places to eat. They saw some tourists, but it was mainly local foot traffic.

Ruby's heart skipped a beat when she saw the sign for Montez's Grill. It was named after Montez Sr., not the Montez she was trying to put out of her mind. She hadn't seen him since Saturday morning, but that didn't matter.

He'd been on her mind ever since their confrontation at the shop. She felt a little bad about calling him an asshole, but she certainly wasn't going to reach out to him. Things were already awkward. They'd both said what they needed to say and she planned to do the mature thing—and just avoid him for the next couple months.

When she pushed the door open she was inundated with laughter, murmured voices, the sound of clinking plates and glasses and subtle Cuban music.

Jaidyn, one of Julieta's cousins, smiled at her as she stepped out from behind the hostess stand. She had on the standard black pants and black T-shirt uniform of the restaurant. "Hey, Ruby."

"Hey, Jules said she called in an order."

"Ah…kitchen's backed up but I've got an empty booth you can wait at."

"Oh, that's okay, I'll just wait up here." She didn't want to take up any seating. Not when it was clear they were busy and could probably use all the space they could get tonight.

A big hand settled on the small of her back, making her jump until she realized it was Montez moving in next to her. He gave her a heated look that made her insides melt just a teeny bit. "I actually asked Julieta to send you down here. There's no takeout waiting and she's going to be headed home soon. Said she'd bring your purse down here once she closed up. Have dinner with me? I'd like to talk to you."

Ruby blinked as she digested his words. "You set this up so we could talk?"

"I figured you'd probably ignore my calls and I wanted to make sure you came."

There was something about the way he said the word 'came' that brought up an altogether *different* mental image. Just like that, her cheeks heated.

He didn't miss the reaction either, if the low, muted groan he gave was any indication. "Say you'll stay," he murmured, his gaze dipping to her mouth.

Unable to find her voice, she simply nodded.

She was barely aware of their surroundings as he guided her to a corner booth with a decent amount of privacy. When she saw a bottle of red wine and two glasses already waiting she nearly stumbled. This was definitely unexpected and incredibly sweet, but she didn't want to get her hopes up too much. She was pretty sure Montez would break her heart if this ended up being some sort of let-Ruby-down-easy type of thing where he told her again he just wanted sex and only sex. But...despite being a cynic, she was pretty sure that wasn't what this was. Even if she was too afraid to hope it was what she'd been wishing for, for a year.

After she sat, he slid in across from her, his dark gaze full of way too many emotions for her to figure out. Lust was a definite one, but...he looked almost nervous too. "I know I apologized Saturday but I'm doing it again."

"You don't have to." Nervously, she traced her finger up and down the stem of the delicate glass.

"I do. I never should have said those things to you. I'm not making excuses, but I want to explain...why I did."

She nodded once, wanting him to continue. "Okay."

"Adjusting to the civilian world was harder than I expected. Way harder. Probably because of this," he said, motioning to the side of his face. She noticed he sat with the scarred side facing the wall. "But even dealing with people I know love and care about me and don't give a crap about my face is still sometimes an adjustment. Cooking and my restaurant and even my crazy family have kept me sane. Then...I met you."

There was a note in his voice she couldn't read. "And that's bad?"

He gave her a wry smile. "Hell no. I wanted you, still want you. But I thought there was never a chance between us. When I got back from Afghanistan..." He scrubbed a hand over his face, looked away for a long moment.

She wanted to reach out and touch him, to comfort him. "You don't have to go on."

"No, it's not..." He pushed out a sigh. "My ex made it clear that I was good enough to fuck but not good enough to be on her arm in public. Ever. She ended things the first night I got home. So when you said all those things to me I wanted to give you an out—and to protect myself from getting burned by you."

His words were raw, real, and broke her heart. And she wanted to punch his ex-girlfriend in the face for ever making him feel inferior. "Montez—"

He cut her off with a sharp shake of his head. "I just need to know if this is some weird...savior complex you have. Like, fuck the scarred guy out of pity. Even saying it out loud I know it sounds fucking stupid," he muttered. "Trust me, I absolutely know it. I just... I don't know why you want me. You're the most beautiful woman I've ever met. I've literally seen men trip over themselves trying to get a better look at you."

She watched him for a long moment, digested everything he'd said and chose her words carefully. "You're one of the nicest, most sincere men I've ever met. Ever. I see the way you treat your mom and sister and yes, even your brothers. God, they're enough to drive anyone crazy. Your brothers, I mean. You're like this solid pillar, the one everyone goes to for advice. And I know how much volunteer work you do down at the VA. Jesus, Montez, how could I not want you?"

For the first time since she'd met him, his cheeks turned crimson. He cleared his throat, embarrassed, but she didn't care. He was such a good man and he needed to know it.

"Since I was fourteen, I looked like this." She motioned down at herself. Yeah, she knew what she looked like. She had a freaking mirror and it would be stupid to deny it. "I had to learn early how to figure out who the assholes of the world are. And despite what I said Saturday, you're not just another asshole. You just hurt me. You're the sweetest man I know—and I wasn't kidding about trying on those naughty nurse costumes." She whispered the last part.

144 | KATIE REUS

Pleasure hummed through her when his cheeks flushed again, but this time for a very different reason.

Before he could respond, his mother, a slightly older version of Julieta, appeared out of nowhere wearing a wraparound leopard print dress and subtle gold jewelry. She smiled at the two of them. "My favorite oldest son," she murmured. She briefly cupped Ruby's cheeks lightly. "And *mi futura nuera*." Her gold bangles jangled as her hands dropped. "Don't worry about a thing. Your appetizer and salads will be out soon."

"Thanks, Mama," Montez murmured as Ruby did the same.

Seleste Mederos simply patted his cheek and winked at Ruby before moving on to another table.

Ruby had seen the woman at work before and she always came out and greeted customers at least once a night. The restaurant was a staple in the neighborhood and it was clear that she and her husband thought of their regulars like family.

Once Seleste was out of earshot, Ruby leaned a little across the table. "What does *nuera* mean?" She'd learned a lot of Spanish since she'd started working with Jules, but some words she couldn't even begin to guess. Not unless Jules used it in everyday conversation.

Montez just lifted a shoulder, his expression unreadable. "I'll tell you later," he said, after a long moment. "But first I want to get back to that nurse costume you brought up."

She laughed, the weight that had been on her chest for days finally lifting. She wasn't sure what kind of future she and Montez had but she sure wanted the chance to find out.

After dinner Montez walked her back to her car, which was parked across the street from the shop. Thankfully Julieta had dropped off her purse so she hadn't had to go back to the shop to get her stuff. Even though it was summer, a cool breeze kicked up as they headed down the sidewalk.

When Montez picked up her hand and slid his fingers through hers, she was pretty sure her heart was about to beat through her chest. She'd never been so excited about a man before. She could admit she was cynical when it came to the opposite sex, but he pretty much blew away all of that.

"I want to take you out again," he murmured as they reached her car.

"I would like that." She turned to face him, glad he was still holding her hand. The hum of excitement punching through her, wondering if he'd kiss her or not, was unbearable.

"I've got to work tomorrow night, but how about Wednesday?"

"Sounds good." Did it ever.

"Pick you up from work?" he murmured, his gaze dropping to her mouth, hunger simmering in his dark eyes.

Ruby nodded, unable to find her voice.

They both leaned in at the same time and when his lips brushed against hers, she saw those clichéd fireworks. A wild energy buzzed through her as he grasped the back of her head and held tight as his tongue teased against hers.

She could totally fall for this man. She'd seen her mother go through loser after loser, had been so adamant that she'd never let a guy close enough to hurt her. Then she'd met Montez and he'd shoved his way right into her heart without even trying.

She nipped his bottom lip, moving closer into his embrace. His erection was thick against her stomach and the feel of it made her groan into his mouth. As she clutched onto his shoulders, he pulled back, his breathing erratic.

"Gotta stop now," he rasped out.

She nodded even if she didn't want him to. But they were in public and yeah, they didn't need to have a crazy make-out session on the side of the street—across from where she worked.

"Call me when you get home," he said. "So I know you made it safe."

"I will. Or I can just text."

"Call. I want to hear your voice."

Pleasure slid through her veins, warming her from the inside out. She wanted to hear his voice too and it touched her that he wanted to know she'd made it home safe. "I will."

He waited until she was in her car and had pulled away before heading back to the restaurant. As soon as she was on the road she slid her Bluetooth earpiece in and called Raegan. She'd thought about calling Jules but wasn't sure how weird it would be to talk to her about Jules's older brother.

"Hey, Ruby," Raegan said, picking up on the second ring.

She couldn't hold back her excitement. "Guess who I just kissed?"

CHAPTER THIRTEEN

Ford covered his surprise at seeing Grant leaning against his truck in the parking lot outside the range. One of the officers on security must have let him through because civilians weren't supposed to be here. His surprise immediately morphed to concern as he realized there was only one reason Grant would be here.

He shoved his sunglasses up on his head, broke into a jog. "What's wrong?" he demanded, coming to stand in front of the former detective. Had something happened to Raegan? He hadn't talked to her in three days, hadn't known what the hell to say to her after seeing her kissing that guy.

Grant pushed up from the truck, and despite wearing a suit, he looked nothing like a typical businessman. He looked a little like a caged animal—and like he wanted to deck Ford right across the face. "I just wanted to make sure you weren't fucking dead." The words were spoken quietly, but there was no mistaking the undercurrent of anger. "Since you apparently cut things off with my cousin like a total douche, without a word. What the hell is the matter with you? If you don't want to be with her, fine, end things like a man. I never expected you to sleep with her and then just stop calling. It's a dick move."

Tension ratcheted up inside him, all his muscles going taut. "Raegan and I are none of your business."

Grant's jaw tightened. "You're right. But you and I are friends. And my very emotional, pregnant wife is upset for Raegan. I overheard them talking. That's the only fucking reason I'm here right now. I really don't want to be having this conversation but...what the hell, dude? I've seen you practically panting after her for a year."

Ford had mistakenly thought he'd done a good job of hiding his feelings for Raegan, but that was beside the point. He rubbed a hand over his face, feeling awkward talking about any of this. "Look, whatever you overheard is wrong. It was casual for Raegan but it wasn't for me. I can't...be with her if she's with someone else."

Some of the anger seemed to subside from Grant as he frowned. "I can't believe I'm having this fucking conversation," he muttered. "But what the hell are you talking about?"

Yeah, Ford couldn't believe it either. "I was out with one of the guys Monday and saw her kissing some guy. I wasn't following her," he tacked on, as if that even needed to be explained. "It was dumb luck I saw and...I'm just not wired that way." Not to mention she'd told him she wouldn't be dating anyone else. He felt like such an idiot. He should have known she was too good to be true.

Grant blinked, as if Ford had truly surprised him. Then his expression hardened. "Monday night she had a business thing and the guy kissed her out of the blue. She was so pissed about it she passed the job off to Athena— but we decided not to do business with him anyway. And not just because it's Raegan. The women who work for Red Stone need to feel safe at work. Need to *be* safe."

At Grant's words, a sinking sensation filled his gut. He'd jumped to the wrong conclusion. He knew why he'd done it. He'd let his past cloud his judgment. "Fuck." Ford wanted to kick his own ass. Repeatedly.

"I've known you a long time, man, so I know your baggage. I get it, especially after what happened with your brother. But..." He shrugged and pulled out his car keys. "Raegan's not like your ex. Not even close. You're a dumbass if you think that." He didn't say anything else, just tapped his key fob and stalked across the parking lot.

Feeling like the biggest dick on the planet, he pulled out his cell phone and called her. It went to her voicemail after two rings, making him think she'd rejected his call. Not that he blamed her. It had been three days since he'd contacted her. He wondered if she'd even listen to him. He had to come clean about his issues, to make her understand why he'd jumped to the wrong conclusion—and apologize because he'd been so wrong to make an assumption like that.

Grant was right; he did have baggage. He *thought* he'd dealt with it, but seeing her kissing someone else had brought up all those feelings of betrayal and inadequacy. And instead of phoning her and confronting her about what he'd seen, he'd walked away without giving her a chance to explain herself.

Instead of calling again, he texted her. *I'm sorry I've been a ghost the past few days. I'd like to see you in person and apologize.* He also wanted to explain everything to her, but texting wasn't the way to do it.

He doubted she'd text him right back or maybe even at all, so he got into his truck and headed home. He'd screwed up because of his own bullshit. Now he might have lost the best thing that had ever happened to him. He'd convinced himself that something would go wrong, then, when he'd thought it had, he hadn't even fought for her.

Losing Raegan because of his own issues was something he knew he'd regret forever. Now he had to make it right.

* * *

"I'm surprised Dominique isn't here tonight," Raegan said to Ruby and Julieta. A group of her girlfriends had come out tonight but Dominique had said she couldn't. In fact, she'd been surprisingly MIA since Saturday's event. She'd been at work, but she'd been acting a little off and hadn't wanted to hang out with anyone.

Before either of them could respond, Lizzy, Porter's wife, snorted from across the big round table. "She's busy with a certain Russian, from what I hear."

Everyone at the table quieted and stared at her.

"Who? What?" Raegan asked. Dominique hadn't dated a man in...well, since Raegan had known her. She was always so quiet about that part of her life. She wondered if it was that Russian from Saturday's event, the one who'd dropped off the security feed of the club to Porter. But Dominique had seemed to hate the guy. That being an understatement.

Lizzy stared at all of them in clear surprise. "Seriously, I'm the only one who knows about this?"

"Apparently," Athena said. "Come on, spill. She's been cagey all week and I need some good gossip."

"No way." Lizzy shook her head. "Dominique is Porter's assistant. If I make her mad she might screw up his schedule or...I can't think of anything else right now, but she can be scary. So nope, no spilling of secrets will be happening." She made a zipping motion across her lips and mimed throwing away the key.

"We'll get it out of you," Julieta said, picking up her own wine glass.

Julieta had known Lizzy since they were kids, but Raegan knew her cousin-in-law well enough that if Lizzy didn't want to talk about something, she wouldn't.

Everyone quieted for a moment as their server dropped off three appetizers and placed them around the big table. Raegan had been working like crazy and going straight home every day this week, thanks to the unknown threat looming over her head. Unfortunately she'd been going home alone because a certain jerk had decided to cut all contact with her. It hurt way more than she'd imagined. She'd thought they had something good, that they were moving in a positive direction. Then he'd just cut all contact.

She mentally shook herself, not even wanting to go there right now. She'd reviewed the video feed from the club and from the event but hadn't seen anyone she recognized or that stood out to her as a threat. And she hadn't received any creepy messages or anything. Still, she was being smart, and the only reason she was even out tonight was because Jules' and Lizzy's significant others were at the bar keeping watch over them while they had a girls' night. She hated that she was the reason for the 'security' but she was glad to get out with her friends. Especially since Ford had pulled the rug out from under her. She hadn't decided whether to text him back or not yet.

"If you want gossip," she said to Athena as everyone started reaching for the appetizers, "guess who just called and texted me after days of radio silence?"

"Ooh, sexy cop is back on the scene?" Ruby asked. The beautiful blonde was happier than Raegan had ever seen her since she'd started dating Montez a few days ago.

"Uh, no." And she didn't know if she even wanted to contact him. She didn't play games, and he'd really hurt her. She started to reach for the crab-stuffed mushrooms when she saw the almost guilty look on Lizzy's face. "What's that look?"

"Nothing."

"You're such a liar. Do you know something about Ford?"

Lizzy shrugged as she scooped a few of the coconut fried shrimp onto her plate. "I know a lot about him. He's been friends with Grant for years."

"Don't be a smart-ass."

"I'm not supposed to say." She picked up a shrimp, nibbled on it as everyone watched her.

"If you don't tell her, I'm going to make you wear the ugliest bridesmaid dress possible. With ruffles and bows and everything you hate. In pink. It'll be a special dress, reserved just for you." Julieta's expression was deadpan as she lifted her glass of wine, her eyebrows raised challengingly.

"Fine…" Lizzy turned back to Raegan, her expression apologetic. "I might have overheard Grant telling Porter that he was going to see Ford today."

Mortification swelled inside Raegan as Lizzy's words settled in. "Oh, my God," she breathed out. She did not need her cousins 'defending her honor' or whatever misguided idea they might have. A little overprotectiveness was fine, but this was nuts.

"I *know*. I told Porter it was a bad idea but apparently Belle is super emotional right now—and I understand. I was crazy emotional when I was pregnant too. But she was really upset for you, was talking about going to see Ford and punching him," Lizzy sighed, "and I quote, 'in his big dumb face.' So…I think Grant might have gone to see him today to make her happy."

Raegan felt her cheeks flush with embarrassment. She'd been ranting to Belle yesterday about Ford's disappearing act but that had just been to release her frustration to a friend. She was a grown woman. She didn't need or want her family getting involved with her fizzled relationship. Hell, it had barely been a relationship. Just sex. At least to Ford. And yeah, that stung pretty deeply because she'd really been into him. "I think I need another glass of wine," she muttered.

"It's probably not as bad as you think," Ruby said, giving her a hopeful expression.

"Yeah, sure." At least now she had her answer as to why Ford had called and texted after days of the silent treatment. She'd really thought they were on the same page. She'd started to think they might have something real together. At least this had happened before she'd really fallen for him.

Who was she kidding—it hurt no matter what. She had absolutely nothing to say to him, especially not since he was only calling because of her cousin.

CHAPTER FOURTEEN

Ford pushed away from the wall when he saw Raegan round the corner from where the elevators were.

She paused when she saw him, her lips pulling into a thin line before she continued toward him.

"How'd you get in the building?" she asked, pulling her key out of her purse. She had on one of those wraparound dresses he'd noticed that she favored. This one was solid black. It highlighted all her curves—not that he should be focusing on that right now. Not when he owed her an apology. Just seeing her made him ache inside, only reminded him how much he'd missed her.

"I was still on your guest list." Which yeah, showing up uninvited was a shitty thing to do, but he wanted to see her, to do this in person. Even if he was pretty sure she never wanted to see him again. But he had to try and make this right. He missed her and wanted another shot.

She crossed her arms over her chest, her expression neutral. "Look, Lizzy told me that Grant might have visited you today so if that's the case, know that I had nothing to do with that. You shouldn't be here because you think you have to apologize for…whatever."

"I do need to apologize…" He trailed off as a couple a few doors down stepped from their condo. They both waved at Raegan, who smiled and waved back.

Sighing, she opened her door. "Let's do this inside," she murmured.

Feeling more nervous than he could ever remember, he trailed after her. He'd screwed up and he knew he'd get one chance to make this right. That meant laying it on the line for Raegan, being totally honest. Even if he didn't want to talk about his past, he knew he needed to.

She didn't go far, just into the entryway. The door shut behind them, but she didn't bother locking it. Just leaned against it, eyeing him warily. "Why are you here?"

"I owe you an apology. I saw you out early Monday evening—completely by chance—kissing the guy from Saturday's event." Her eyes widened and she started to protest but he shook his head. "I now know that you weren't kissing him, that he kissed you. Not that it's an excuse for me just falling off the face of the earth like I did. I'm sorry for the radio silence." He shoved his hands in his pockets, trying to get a read on her, but for once he couldn't tell what she was thinking.

He hated that there was now a wall between them— and that it was his fault. He hated that he'd hurt her. That he'd misjudged her.

"So you saw me kissing some guy, or what you thought was me kissing some guy, and decided to just...not ask me about it?" Hurt filled her blue eyes, making him feel worse.

"I should have asked you about it. Hell, I shouldn't have jumped to conclusions." From where he'd sat, it had looked like a pretty intense kiss, but he hadn't looked that long. Hadn't wanted to. He'd let his past get in the way, blur his judgment. He knew that now and was afraid he'd screwed up the best thing that had happened to him.

"Why didn't you?"

He drew a deep breath and came clean. "I was scared of your answer."

She made a scoffing sound, which he figured he deserved. "You were scared?"

"I..." He cleared his throat. "Years ago I was with a woman who was cheating on me. A lot, I found out later. I ignored my instinct because I was hung up on her. I thought I loved her. So when she said she was working late or told me I was paranoid, I believed her. I've never been the jealous type and she made me feel fucking nuts for questioning her. For questioning what my instinct was telling me."

He took another deep breath, hated admitting this at all. He still couldn't believe how stupid he'd been.

"Turns out she was sleeping with my brother. Things got really messy for a while, especially after Dallas proposed to her. She left him a month before their wedding. He'd been on a fast track to a partnership with one of the biggest firms in Miami, but when that didn't happen, she split." Ford had thought he'd feel some sort of vindication or happiness, but instead he'd felt bad for his brother. Dallas had lost his job and the woman he'd loved, no matter how horrible she was, in the span of days.

Raegan's defensive pose dissipated and she dropped her arms from around herself. Sighing, she hung her purse on the hook by the front door, slipped off her heels and locked the door. "Come on, let's finish this conversation in the kitchen. It sounds like you need a beer."

Even though he was surprised, he didn't question her as he followed after her. Since she lived in a condo, her kitchen was relatively small, but there was a built-in bar top with stools on the outside of her actual kitchen. She pointed over the bar top for him to sit as she went to the refrigerator.

"So, you decided to lump me in with your ex?" she asked as she pulled out two beers. She handed him one as she popped the top of her own.

He fought the urge to squirm. "Yeah."

"That's pretty stupid."

He scrubbed a hand over his face. "I know."

She leaned against the bar top opposite him, watching him carefully. "You just fell off the face of the earth. It was...hurtful. We shared some pretty intense sex, and then nothing from you. And I'll admit, it was more than just sex for me. I missed you." She looked so damn vulnerable as she said it. "Even if you thought I'd been kissing someone else—and I can understand you being annoyed after we'd had that talk about not seeing other people—you could have *asked* me about it."

"I know. I should have. And I know words are bullshit, but I really am sorry. You deserve better than the way I acted. For the record, I've missed you too."

She continued to watch him carefully, as if debating something. "I should be a lot madder at you right now, but okay."

His heart rate kicked up. "Okay?"

"Okay, I forgive you. Only because I know you've been checking in with Porter about my whole 'stalker' situation—or whatever's going on—and I can tell you're being sincere. And okay, that story…" Her eyes widened a little. "Seriously, your brother? Then she got engaged to him? Holy awkward Thanksgiving dinners."

He let out a wry laugh, the tension in his chest easing. "Yeah, it's why things are still strained between us."

"How long ago was this?"

"About two years."

"No wonder you have trust issues." He snorted at that, but she just continued. "I can't be with someone who cuts all contact like that, so if you do it again, we're done. I don't play relationship games, and I like you, Ford. I…I'm going to let this go, but I just can't deal with something like this again. If you have a problem with anything, talk to me. Okay?"

He was surprised she was giving him a second chance at all, realized how lucky he was, but he nodded. "I will."

"And…I'm just going to say it so we're on the same page. I like a little possessiveness but I need to be with someone who trusts me. I'll trust you unless you give me a reason not to."

"That's fair. But I can only show you that going forward." And he planned to.

She nodded once. "Okay. So…want to pop a pizza in the oven and watch a movie? I was out with friends earlier but only munched on some appetizers and I'm still starving."

Warmth glowed in his chest, a huge weight lifting off him. Being able to spend the evening with her was a gift he could hardly believe he deserved after what he'd done. "Yeah. I'll put the pizza in if you want to pick a movie."

"Oh, I think I get to pick the next five movies." Her grin was just a little wicked as she said it.

He couldn't help but grin back. "Is that right?"

"Yep. Call it part of your apology."

His gaze fell to her mouth and hunger surged through him. Everything about her got him hot. He'd been trying not to think about her the last three days, but had failed. She shouldn't be letting him off the hook so easily, but he wasn't going to question his luck. "I can think of some other ways to make it up to you." He dropped his voice, the intent in his words clear. But he didn't want to simply jump back into sex, not after he'd screwed up so bad.

Her cheeks tinged pink. "If these ways involve you naked with your head between my legs, I'll allow it."

He groaned at the description. She'd been pretty quiet during their many bouts of sex, definitely not a dirty talker like him, but this…was fucking hot. He cleared his throat as his cock hardened, and just nodded. For once, he couldn't find his voice. All he wanted to do right now was just what she'd said.

But he also wanted to show her that this thing between them was more than just physical. Because he was playing for keeps with Raegan.

CHAPTER FIFTEEN

As he reached Raegan's office, his heart rate increased as it always did. His hands shook as he approached her desk. She wasn't there but he could see her crossed legs where she was sitting in her boss's office and could hear them talking.

They'd ordered lunch in today, something they only did about once a week. He took their boxed lunches off his cart and set them both on Raegan's desk. "Lunch," he called out, excitement humming through him as he waited to see her.

But the other woman, Athena, stepped out instead and smiled at him. "Hey, Teo. How much do we owe you?"

He was momentarily disappointed that it was just Athena, that Raegan wouldn't be coming out as well. Normally it was Raegan—she was the assistant, after all. But maybe she was working on something. It couldn't be that she didn't want to see him. Could it?

He curbed the anger that sliced through him, forced a smile for Athena. "Ah, sixteen ninety-five."

Smiling, she handed him a twenty. "Keep the change."

He nodded, murmuring thanks as she picked up the boxes and headed back into her office. Because of the angle he could only see Raegan's legs but he could hear typing. Maybe on her laptop. The must be why she hadn't come out. It had nothing to do with him.

Still...he wanted to see her. Was desperate to get a glimpse. He kept wondering if she'd remembered him from Friday night. But if she had, the police would have already come to see him.

He pretended to readjust the other boxed lunches for this floor in the hopes he'd get a glimpse of her.

"You can put that down for a few minutes," Athena said.

He watched as a laptop slid into his view, moving to the edge of the desk. So she had been working. It didn't ease his tension any. Some days he kept his food truck open longer just to get a peek of her leaving work, but the last week he hadn't seen her coming or going. He'd still been reading all her texts but they didn't tell him much other than she'd been in some argument with one of the guys she was screwing. Which was good.

He took a deep breath. He wouldn't think about her being with anyone else right now. It would just upset him. Soon enough she'd see that she was meant for him, no one else. He could forgive her if she was sorry enough.

"...dress fitting tomorrow. Supposed to be over by two."

"You'll have to tell me what La Boutique Bellissima is like. I've got an appointment scheduled there in two weeks to talk with the owner."

Teo knew he'd been lingering long enough as it was and pushed his three-tiered cart out into the hall. He'd gotten so much more than he imagined today. He knew that bridal boutique, had set up his food truck in the area on multiple occasions.

Red Stone Security was one of the only places he did actual deliveries to. Until a few months ago he hadn't even done the deliveries himself. One of his part-time employees hadn't been feeling well so he'd let him take over the food truck while he'd finished the deliveries personally. It was how he'd met Raegan for the first time.

Beautiful, vibrant Raegan.

Now that he knew where she was going to be tomorrow he'd be able to get there before her. He wouldn't even have to track her using her phone. He'd still check it, of course, but it was better for him to set up early and check out potential spots to take her from if the opportunity should arise.

He'd head down to the area later tonight, look for any security cameras in the vicinity. He could disable some and break others.

For once, it seemed fate was on his side. He had an advantage over her this time. It would give him the element of surprise. Grabbing her in broad daylight was a risk, but if he could get her alone he'd do it.

Soon she'd be all his. Once he made her understand that he was in charge, that she belonged to him, things would be good again. The burning anger inside him would be manageable again. At this point he almost didn't care about someone seeing him. He just needed to be with her, to have her. If he couldn't have her, no one could.

CHAPTER SIXTEEN

"Is it normal for guys to come to these fittings?" Ford asked Montez and Ivan, who were sitting on the bench next to him.

They were outside the bridal shop after Julieta had kicked Ivan out "for inappropriate suggestions," as she put it.

Ford understood why Ivan was there, even if he wouldn't be allowed to see Julieta try on her wedding dress. And Montez was Julieta's brother—though he was clearly only there because Ruby was. But Ford had never thought guys came to these kinds of things. He'd have been shadowing Raegan regardless, but she'd asked him before he could suggest it. He hadn't wanted to ask her if it was normal for significant others to be here and reveal how truly relationship-challenged he was. He'd grown up with a brother and most of his friends were either cops or retired Marines. And his ex hadn't had many girlfriends so this was new territory.

Ivan just shrugged as Montez nodded. "Yeah, things are different now, man. Women want their men involved in *all* of the wedding stuff. They've even got couples showers."

Wait...couples showers? He blinked, trying to figure out what Montez meant. Was that like a swingers thing?

It seemed too weird for Montez to be talking about casually. God, he really felt old.

Montez burst out laughing, shaking his head. "Oh my God, not like that. I see where your mind just went. Showers, like for babies and weddings and stuff. Not all guys go and not all of them are joint, but yeah, it's a thing now. Trust me, I've got a lot of female cousins. You're gonna be expected to go to all sorts of stuff like this now."

Ford didn't think that sounded like a bad thing, not if he got to hang out with Raegan more. Just maybe not all the time. Baby showers didn't sound like fun. "Those drinks inside were fucking awesome," he said, referring to whatever the hell they'd given them in the shop earlier. It was bubbly and had fruit in it and he wouldn't be caught dead drinking it anywhere else, but damn.

"We'd still be drinking them if someone hadn't got us kicked out," Montez muttered.

Ford nodded, looking at Ivan. "I think you horrified the sales clerk, talking about making sure her wedding dress had an easy access—"

"Dude, I do not need to hear that again." Montez stood, shooting Ivan a pointed look. "She's still my sister. Keep some shit to yourself."

Ivan just grinned and shrugged again, which seemed pretty standard for the guy's communication style.

Montez rolled his eyes before nodding at the café next door. "I'm gonna grab a drink. You guys want something?"

Ford stood as Ivan said, "Iced coffee."

"I'll go with you." He wanted to stretch his legs and he needed to use the restroom. And Raegan had said it would take at least another hour for them to finish getting fitted. "You gonna go anywhere?" he asked Ivan, needing to know that someone would stay put in front of the store.

"Nope."

He nodded once. The guy was a former Ranger and he worked for Red Stone. Not to mention he'd been there the other night at the club and knew the deal with Raegan right now. Nothing had happened in the last week—no threats, no phone calls, no weird messages or attempted attacks.

But...his gut told him it wasn't random. Not after the things the unknown guy had said to her in that bathroom. It was just too personal. He knew the detective who'd been assigned her case, but the truth was, she wasn't a priority to the department.

Even with some of the guys at Red Stone working on finding out who'd tried to hurt her, they hadn't found much. They hadn't been able to get a matchup of faces from both the club and the event. When people wore hats or hoodies or anything that obscured their faces, it messed with the facial recognition software, making it virtually useless.

It wasn't like she was receiving strange messages they could track either. Which was good and bad. Maybe she didn't really have a stalker. Or maybe the guy who drugged her was just very patient.

That scared Ford more than anything. Someone who was patient was a bigger threat. They'd be less likely to make a mistake.

He rolled his shoulders once and glanced up and down the street as they reached the door to the café. There was a tingling sensation between his shoulder blades.

It put him even more on edge, made him wonder if he was being paranoid, but he'd seen enough combat to never ignore his instinct. Right then he needed to see Raegan, needed to know that she was okay.

"Hey, I'm gonna go talk to Raegan. I'll meet you back outside," he said to Montez. "Get me a bottled water?" he asked, pulling out his wallet.

Montez nodded and waved away his money.

A cool breeze rushed over him, making the wind chimes outside the boutique next door jingle as he reached the glass door to the bridal shop. He smiled at the sight of Raegan on the other side, already starting to push it open.

"Hey," he said, opening it for her.

"Hey, you," she murmured, lifting up on her toes to brush her lips over his. He covered a groan as she stepped back.

She gave him a wide smile and he could tell she was a little tipsy. The women had been drinking mimosas during the fitting and he knew she hadn't eaten much for breakfast that morning.

"Are you done?"

She nodded then glanced around him. "Jules said you can come back in if you're good."

Ivan just laughed but gave Ford a pointed look. One that clearly asked if he wanted backup right now.

Ford shook his head and held the door open again as Ivan stepped past them. He was armed and he'd been well trained.

"Can we grab something to eat really quick? I have a small buzz going and I'm starving," Raegan said. "I was the first done so we've got some time."

He wrapped his arm around her shoulders. After the second chance she'd given him, he wasn't letting her go. He knew he'd let his past cloud his judgment, but the way she'd truly let everything go told him everything he needed to know about her. "Sure, let's head next door."

"Can we head to the food truck instead? I've been to that one before and they've got amazing veggie empanadas."

"Sounds good. I'll snag one too." Out of habit he scanned their surroundings as they waited to cross the street.

There were half a dozen people in line across the street, waiting. He could see them looped down the sidewalk from their angle. A female couple walking a small dog was approaching from the right, but he couldn't see to the left of the food truck. He didn't like it, but he knew that Raegan couldn't live in a bubble.

Besides, he was with her. He'd do anything to keep her safe. As they reached the other side, he was relieved to see nothing out of the ordinary on the other side of the truck. A few benches occupied by people eating food from the truck. It was a typical, sunny Florida day. Everything seemed normal.

Raegan half nuzzled her face against his chest as they got in line. "What's going on in that sexy head of yours?" she murmured.

He laughed lightly, kissing the top of her head. "You are definitely tipsy right now."

"Mmm hmm," she agreed. "And I think we need to head straight back to your place after the fitting."

"Is that right?" he asked quietly. The two college-aged guys in front of them were talking to each other—loudly—about how drunk they'd gotten the night before, and how they needed hangover food. Definitely not a threat.

"Yep. I only got to see it that once. God, that feels like a lifetime ago." She seemed to sober at the comment.

"Yeah." It really did. "I hate what happened, but for the record, I'm glad it brought you into my life."

She looked up at him, eyebrows raised. "I was sorta already in your life."

He grinned. "Yeah. But I was still figuring out how to ask you out."

"Afraid of my cousins?"

He snorted. "More like afraid of you."

She blinked in true surprise, then that slightly wicked smile he loved spread across her face. "I've been told I'm quite scary."

He snorted again. "I'm sure." That word was pretty much the opposite of her. He'd just been a coward. Never again though. He'd let his past hold him back for too long. And deep down…he knew Raegan was it for him. It was that gut instinct. She'd knocked him on his ass and he was never letting her go. Yeah, it was too soon to make any declarations or be completely positive about their future, but he saw the writing on the wall. He knew where this was going. The fact that he was actually looking forward to going to couples showers with her was a pretty big indicator that she was damn special.

Only a couple more people to go now, he realized. When he made eye contact with the man behind the flipped down metal counter, he gave a polite smile, nodded. The guy didn't smile back, barely acknowledged him.

Ford kept his expression neutral, slid his sunglasses over his eyes as he scanned their surroundings again. "You said you've been to this food truck before?" he murmured.

She shifted slightly against him. "Oh, yeah. It's parked right on our street outside work. I bet the owner does crazy-good business, considering the area. Red Stone even opened it up to him to do deliveries a couple months ago."

"So you know the owner, personally?" Ford kept his voice low.

She shrugged against him. "Not really. I mean, we say hi, you know, the normal polite stuff. He delivers to Athena and me once a week along with our whole floor. I don't know of any food trucks that add that type of extra service. It's pretty great."

Ford's radar was going nuts as the guy continued to shoot looks at him and Raegan. The guy's body language was all wrong. All his muscles were pulled tight as he continued taking orders and preparing food. Ford was surprised no one was in there with him. He also wondered about the location of the truck. He knew that food trucks moved around a city, but he didn't like that this was the same one that parked outside Red Stone, and just happened to be at this location at the same time Raegan had a dress fitting here. Or that the owner had access to Raegan's office, to her at work. No, it was time to get her the hell out of here.

He didn't care if he was being paranoid, he was going with his gut. "You trust me?"

Raegan straightened next to him. "Uh, yeah. Of course."

"We're going to head back across the street to the bridal boutique. Stay to the left of me."

"Okay." There was a note of concern in her voice, but she didn't say anything else as they broke away from the line.

A sense of relief had already started pulsing through him as they headed back toward the street and away from the food truck. He didn't want to pull his weapon out in full view of everyone but as soon as they stepped down onto the curb, rounding the back of food truck, he reached behind his back for his pistol.

Just as the back door to the truck flew open.

A muscular man about five feet, ten inches tall was holding a pistol directly at Ford, his dark eyes glittering with hatred. Barely four feet separated them. He'd never survive a direct shot this close. It didn't matter how much training and experience he had, he couldn't draw fast enough to shoot someone who had a weapon pointed directly at him only feet away. Maybe on television that shit worked.

Everything slowed down in that instant as he stared down the barrel of the weapon. He wanted to shove Raegan behind him, but she'd clutched onto him tighter and he didn't want to make any sudden moves.

"Get your hands off her," the man snarled. "Raegan, get in the back of the truck."

There were gasps coming from people on the sidewalk and someone said "Gun," before running away. Ford could see other people scattering in his periphery but all his focus was on this threat.

"I'm going to take my arm from around her," Ford said slowly, moving just as slowly. Adrenaline surged through him, but he forced himself to remain calm. No sudden movements, nothing to spook the guy into shooting her. There was no way in hell he was letting her get in that truck, however, but one step at a time. "You don't really want to shoot anyone. You haven't done anything you can't take back yet."

The man's hand shook, his eyes just a little wild. "I'll shoot you right fucking here! I know you were going to take her away from me! You think I'm stupid?"

"Please don't shoot." Raegan's voice trembled but her words were clear.

The man's focus lasered in on her even though he didn't move his weapon in her direction. Thank God. "Didn't I tell you to get in the truck?" he snarled. "Why'd you come over here today? Just to show off that you're with him? I know what you want and I'm going to give it to you. Get in the fucking truck!"

A siren wailed in the distance, cutting through the air and making Raegan jump. The man turned at the sound, as if on instinct. His weapon hand wavered to the side. Not by much, but it was enough.

Ford knew this might be the only chance he ever got. He had to take it.

Years of training had prepared him for this moment. It would take too many steps to draw his weapon, bring it around his body and fire at the threat. No, he had to go with the only other option.

Adrenaline punching through him, he shoved Raegan to the side as he lunged at the man. Since the guy was raised up on the back of the truck, Ford rammed into the guy's upper legs and lower torso with a full-on tackle.

A shot boomed through the air as Ford slammed him to the floor. He heard the clatter of the weapon but couldn't see where it had gone as the guy screamed.

The man punched at Ford's head. He ducked to the side, the blow glancing his temple.

He struck out with his fist, slamming it against the guy's nose. Bone crunched under the force of his punch as the man's head slammed back against the metal floor.

Ford needed to take complete control of the situation, disable the threat. Everything else around him funneled out as that thought took over. He wasn't even sure if Raegan had been hit by that bullet and he couldn't risk looking out the door, couldn't take his focus off this man.

Fear and rage surged through him that she might have been injured, or worse. He slammed his elbow across the guy's face, breaking more bones.

The man cried out in pain, blood gushing out his nose as he punched at Ford's middle. Either he had training or he was just jacked up on adrenaline—or drugs—to keep fighting with broken bones.

His fist landed against Ford's ribcage, once, twice—*Slam*! Ford landed another face shot. When the guy's head thumped back against the floor again, his entire body went limp.

Not taking a chance that the guy wasn't out, Ford rolled him onto his stomach and yanked his wrists together behind his back. At a shuffling sound, he went to reach for his weapon but stilled when he saw Montez coming in through the front of the truck, his expression fierce and a weapon in his hand. He briefly wondered if Montez had a concealed permit, then dismissed the thought. He didn't give a shit right now.

"Raegan?" Ford rasped out.

"Okay," Montez answered.

Relief nearly overwhelmed him, but he shoved it back down. "I need something to secure him," he said as Montez moved into action, rummaging around the small kitchen.

Spicy scents teased the air as he suddenly realized the sirens were growing even louder in the distance. "Anyone get shot?"

"No." Montez hurried over with a type of bungee cord. "I saw what was happening as I came out of the café across the street. Ivan must have seen it from inside the shop."

Ford nodded, securing the man's wrists as Montez continued to talk.

"Ivan had to carry Raegan across the street. She didn't want to leave you. But she's fine, man. Completely unharmed. Someone saved us the trouble of calling the cops too. They should be here soon."

If those sirens were any indication, Ford guessed fewer than sixty seconds. "Got something for his feet?" he asked as the man started to groan softly. Ford kept his knee firmly against the asshole's back. He resisted the urge to hurt the guy more as the words the man had thrown at Raegan replayed in his mind. 'I know what you want and I'm going to give it to you.' He could just imagine what the fucker had planned for her. A shudder racked him, but he tightened his control.

Seconds later Montez was back with white zip ties. "We use these at my place for chill bags."

Ford just grunted, grabbed a handful of the ties. He secured the man's feet, then his hands again for good measure, making sure they were double-tied. Heart racing, he looked up at Montez. "Will you—"

"Go. I got this."

Ford was glad he didn't have to waste time with words, that Montez understood he needed to see for himself that Raegan was unharmed.

He jumped down from the food truck, immediately saw a giant hole in the back of a silver car. Bullet hole.

The relief that surged through him was almost too much when he saw Raegan on the other side of the street behind the glass doors of the bridal shop. Her eyes were wide as she stared at him, one hand pressed to the glass.

Ivan was next to her, his hand on her shoulder. More people lined the windows, staring out in horror, but he only had eyes for her.

After looking for oncoming vehicles, he raced across the street, his heart thundering in his chest. He just needed to hold her. He'd made it halfway across when she shoved Ivan's hand off and pushed the door open.

As he reached the sidewalk edge she threw herself at him, a sob escaping. "Ford! I thought…" Her words were garbled as she buried her face in his neck.

He was unable to say anything as he held her tight. Probably too tight, but she didn't complain. "You need to wait inside," he finally managed to rasp out, still holding onto her. The subtle vanilla scent of her shampoo wrapped around him, grounded him. She was okay, he repeated to himself. She was unharmed and in his arms. She wasn't going anywhere.

And the threat to her was down. That was what was important. Ford was going to find out everything there was to know about that bastard and make sure he never got the chance to hurt anyone again.

She shook her head against his neck. "Not leaving you."

At the sound of the sirens screaming down the street he turned, saw a line of police cars coming. But he still didn't let her go.

They'd face this together. The way he intended to face everything life had to throw at them from now on.

CHAPTER SEVENTEEN

Raegan was exhausted, but at least she wasn't still shaking out of control. She'd thought she'd never feel normal again. Still didn't. Not really.

Everything about earlier today was too surreal. The way Ford had taken on that guy with a gun like a real-life superhero, the way he'd just tackled him.

It was…God, she didn't even know. The only thing she did know was that she'd never get that image out of her head as long as she lived. She'd been terrified for him. Then Ivan had appeared out of nowhere and carried her away like a linebacker. He'd moved with such precision and speed, clearly just as trained as Ford.

Ford squeezed her hand and she realized she'd zoned out. "What?"

"Detective Duarte asked if there was anything else you wanted to add," he murmured.

They were sitting in the detective's office in front of his desk. "No, I'm just glad this is all over. I can't believe he cloned my phone. It's so…" There were too many words. *Invasive, horrifying…* She shuddered. "Are you sure he won't be getting out?"

The detective gave her a sharp, satisfied grin. "Yes. And I don't get to say that nearly as often as I'd like, but he won't even be eligible for bail. Not after what we've found at his house."

She shuddered again, was so grateful for the Miami PD—and Ford. Once Teo King had been arrested, they'd searched his house and discovered an insulated, padded room with a bed and hundreds of pictures of her covering all the walls. Not only that, but boxes of pictures of her by herself and with friends, taken over the last couple months. Right about the time he'd started delivering to Red Stone Security.

But that wasn't the reason he'd be going away. The police had discovered a body buried in his backyard, and considering the social security checks coming in for his mother—who hadn't been seen by any neighbors in months—they were pretty sure it was her. No doubt it was a murder, not with the bullet holes in her skull. Something Raegan didn't want to think about.

"Can I go home, then?"

The detective nodded. "Yes. For what it's worth, you were lucky. This guy...he's been flying under the radar but now that we know who he is, we're going to rip his life apart, see if there have been more victims. Anything we can charge him with, we will. No matter what, he's already going down for his crimes. And we're taking an-other look at that club's security feed from the night you were drugged."

"Thank you. For everything." She kept questioning herself, wondering if there had been signs. But the guy had never asked for her phone number, never shown any interest. Not that she'd been aware of. She hated that she was questioning herself, but was just glad this nightmare was over and everyone had come out unscathed. She tried to banish the image of Ford tackling that lunatic but it kept replaying in her mind.

As they stood, Ford looked at the detective. "Give us a few minutes before we head out?"

The detective nodded and quietly exited his own office.

Raegan guessed the reason he'd asked for privacy was because all her family and friends were waiting for them in the lobby of the PD. They hadn't cared that it would take hours to make a statement and deal with answering a hundred questions. They'd all descended on the police department, and according to Lizzy, the only person she'd talked to as of yet, no one was leaving until they saw her.

"This is a stupid question, but how're you feeling?" Ford asked, his big hands settled protectively on her hips.

She placed her hands on his chest, glad she had him to lean on. "Tired and hungry. And I'm pretty sure I should be asking you that question."

He blinked as if she'd surprised him. "I'm okay."

"I was so scared for you. You just...went at him like a battering ram. It all happened so fast." Trembles racked her body and she hated that she seemed more affected than him and he was the one who'd taken on a guy with a gun. "How are you so okay about this?" Maybe he wasn't. Maybe he was just putting on a good show.

"I hate that you had to witness that violence, that an asshole could have killed you, but that's not the first time I've faced down a loaded weapon."

Her fingers clutched his shirt. "That's not making me feel any better."

His smile was wry. "I just mean I've had training—the best in the world—and experience. First in the Corps, then with the PD. If you want to talk to someone about what happened, I know some people."

She shrugged, not sure she needed or wanted to talk to anyone other than him. But she said, "Thanks. You ready to face my family?"

He let out a short laugh. "Yeah, but after they see you're okay, we're heading back to my place and not leaving for a couple days. I took off Monday already and I've told Porter you're not coming in either."

She blinked. "Seriously?"

He nodded. "Yep. Porter wants you to take off all of next week, but I figured you'd shoot him down pretty fast."

"You really do know me," she murmured. "Taking Monday off seems like a good plan though." Definitely not something she'd say no to. Especially not since it would mean nonstop sex with Ford. At least if she had anything to say about it.

After brushing his lips over hers, he slung an arm around her shoulders. "Let's get out of here."

Leaning into him, she knew without a doubt that this was a man she could depend on for anything. When she'd thought she might lose him she'd realized that her feelings for him were way more than 'like.' "Ford, I'm falling for you. Pretty hard." Saying the words was terrifying. She'd never been in love before and she was pretty sure she was fast on her way to being just that if she wasn't already.

"I'm falling for you too. And I'm pretty sure I'm not letting you go." His words were raspy and his voice steady.

Her heart flipped over in her chest. "I'm not letting you go either."

* * *

"Thank you for waiting at the police station," Ruby said as Montez pulled into her driveway.

He snorted. "Like I'd have left." After making an official statement, he'd waited along with the whole crowd of people for Ford and Raegan to wrap everything up. It had been a madhouse down there. He hated crowds for the most part, but not staying hadn't been an option. "That was some crazy shit," he muttered, turning the ignition off.

"No kidding." Ruby unstrapped her seatbelt, but didn't make a move to get out. Instead she turned to him. "Will you stay the night? I don't...want to be alone tonight."

They'd been exclusive for a week, but hadn't slept together. He wanted to, obviously, but he was going to do things right with Ruby. Because he was pretty sure she was the one for him. Had been sure for a long damn time. He just hadn't wanted to admit it. He and Ruby had had the 'safe sex' talk a couple days ago. He knew she was on the pill and hadn't been with anyone in over a year. And they'd both been tested since their last lovers.

But he'd noticed she hadn't said anything about sex tonight, just asked him to stay. He wasn't surprised she was shaken up. It didn't matter that they read about or saw shootings on the news all the time. Being in close proximity to one—that her friend was involved in—was terrifying for anyone. He'd seen his share of combat but she certainly hadn't, so if he could make her feel safe by staying, he would. "Of course."

Her whole body relaxed at that, the relief rolling off her almost palpable.

"You hungry? I'll whip us up something."

She grinned as she opened her door. "Having a chef boyfriend definitely has some perks."

"Only some?" He got out with her, shutting his door behind him. He liked the sound of the word boyfriend.

"You need your ego stroked?" she murmured, meeting him halfway around the vehicle.

He bit his tongue, grunted a non-response, even though he wanted to suggest she could stroke something else. *Dios*, even the thought of her hands on his cock had him getting hard. But that wasn't what tonight was about. He knew she just didn't want to be alone. Because if she wanted more, he knew Ruby would flat-out tell him. He adored that about her.

She gave him a cheeky grin as they reached her front door and he couldn't believe how nervous he was. Which was stupid. He was a grown man, but since getting out of the Corps he hadn't been with anyone since his bitch of an ex. He'd had a few offers, but…those had felt more like pity fucks. So his hand had done well enough.

"You mind if I change out of this? My feet are killing me." She didn't turn around as she disabled the alarm then reset it.

"No problem. I'll see what you've got in your fridge."

She laughed, giving him a brief kiss before heading to the stairs. "I'm embarrassed to say there's not much. We might have to do takeout."

"I'll be able to work with whatever you've got," he said, watching the fine sway of her ass as she headed up the stairs. He tried not to imagine her stripping off her sexy summer dress and heels but failed.

Slow, he reminded himself. Tonight wasn't about him. She was just scared to be alone.

When he opened her refrigerator he frowned. She hadn't been kidding. A carton of eggs, some funky-colored stuff in a container that he was definitely not opening, yogurt, and bottles of water. After looking at the yogurt he realized the little cartons were expired.

"Takeout it is," he murmured, rummaging around in her drawers until he found a thick pile of takeout menus. He laughed at the stack. She must never cook.

"Find anything you like?"

Montez turned at the sound of Ruby's voice—and dropped all of the takeout menus to the floor.

His brain short-circuited as he saw her standing there in what was most definitely one of the 'naughty nurse' costumes she'd talked about. This wasn't a Halloween type of thing though. No way in hell could she ever go out in public wearing it.

The low-cut minidress was sheer white with red trim and a red and white cross over each nipple. Not that the crosses did anything to cover her up. He could see every delicious inch of her through the dress, including the tight buds of her nipples. Her high heels were ruby red and her little nurse hat had a red and white cross on it as well.

Her grin was wicked when his gaze finally landed on her face. "So? What do you think?"

He made a strangled sound since he couldn't find his voice. *Fuck me.* The reality of her eclipsed any fantasy he'd ever had. The two things were in different stratospheres.

She placed her hands on her hips. "I've got another one upstairs. Want me to try that one on for comparison?"

Her question jerked him back to reality. It would require her leaving and he didn't want that.

Wordlessly he strode across the kitchen, cupped the back of her head in a hard grip and crushed his mouth down on hers. He wasn't letting her get away.

Ever.

She arched against him, moaning into his mouth as she clutched his shoulders. It took him a second to realize what she planned as she hoisted herself up, wrapping her legs around his waist.

He grabbed her ass and hurried out of the kitchen. Bed. He needed to find a bed. Or a flat surface other than the floor.

She bit his bottom lip before nuzzling along his jaw, her little kisses and nips making him even harder. Something he hadn't thought possible.

But Ruby, the sweetest, sexiest woman he knew, was half-naked in his arms. And he was pretty damn sure he loved her. Had known for a while.

When they reached the top of the stairs she slid her hand between their bodies, cupped his erection. He tried to keep his balance but his brain short-circuited yet again.

He started to trip, half turned so that she ended up splayed on top of him on the landing.

Her blonde hair fell loose around her face in waves, the little nurse hat askew as she looked down at him. Her hand was still cupping him and he could see the wicked glint in her gaze, knew that she liked making him crazy.

He also knew she wanted him to take control, if one of their previous conversations and his interactions with her were anything to go by.

He grasped her wrist, pulled it away as he shifted so she was under him. Cupping her cheek, he devoured her mouth. He wanted to go slow, ordered himself to, but when his lips touched hers this time it was as if he lost all ability to reason.

But he forced himself to pull back, to slow down. He wanted to make this good for her, make it as sexy and hot as whatever fantasies she'd spun about him in her head. "Put your hands above your head," he rasped out. He didn't have anything to restrain her hands with—this time. But from what he knew of the little minx, that would be coming soon enough.

Stretched out on the landing, she did as he said without hesitation. The action pushed her breasts out more. They strained against the sheer material. He wanted to rip it away, but he was going to savor this. Savor her.

His cock pulsed once. *Dios*, this woman was going to be the death of him, he was sure. Sitting back on his knees, he drank in the sight of her splayed out for him.

Reaching back, he lifted one of her ankles, brought her leg up and gently kissed her soft skin. She jerked slightly at that brief contact.

Sensitive.

He slid her heel off, heard it clatter behind him in the foyer. Did the same to her other shoe. Keeping his gaze pinned to hers, he moved her feet so they slid over his shoulders. Her breathing grew erratic as he leaned down closer, closer, spreading her thighs for him.

He'd been able to see she wasn't wearing anything under the little minidress earlier, but when he tore his gaze from her face, lasered in on her sweet pussy, he saw just how wet she was for him. "Open wider for me," he ordered.

Groaning, she spread her legs farther. She had just a bit of fine, soft blonde hair covering her mound. The smell of her arousal killed most of his control.

He buried his face between her legs, stroking his tongue up her slick folds.

"Montez." His name came out a choked moan.

And it sounded like pure heaven.

She slid her fingers through his hair, gripped his head tight as he flicked his tongue over her clit. "Oh...yeah." She rolled her hips against his face, the hottest thing he'd ever experienced, as she completely lost herself to pleasure. Her heels dug into his back, made him glad he'd taken the shoes off as she arched up against his mouth, going wild as he increased the pressure.

She was damn reactive.

His cock kicked against his pants as she dug her fingers tighter against his head.

"I'm close." Her words were strangled, unsteady.

He teased her slick entrance, slid two fingers inside her—and she started coming. Her inner walls clenched around him so he added a third finger, never letting up on her clit.

He continued stroking as she came against his tongue, her words garbled nonsense. Which, yeah, made him feel ten fucking feet tall. He loved that she'd come apart for him so easily, wanted to make her do it again.

And again. It would never be enough. Not with Ruby.

When she finally said something that sounded a lot like "Stop," he lifted his head to see her looking at him with a dazed expression. Even so, she reached for his pants.

He let her unbuckle him as he slid the straps of her dress down. His hands actually shook as he bared her to him. The breasts he'd been fantasizing about for too damn long were utter perfection, her tight little nipples a pale pink.

He sucked one into his mouth as she completely freed him. He'd gone commando today, like usual, and was glad for it as she stroked his cock once, twice, three times.

He bit down gently on her nipple, causing her to cry out with what he knew was pleasure. He wished he had more hands because he wanted to touch her everywhere, kiss her all over. And never stop.

"In me, now," she demanded, the words more pleading than anything.

He couldn't force his voice to work, but he lifted his head, positioned himself at her entrance. He was glad they'd already had the talk, that he could slide into her bare this first time. Every time. He didn't want any barriers between them. Ever.

He kept his eyes pinned to hers, grasped her hips as he thrust inside her.

He wanted to kiss her, for her to taste herself on him, but this first time, he wanted to watch her as she came again. And she damn sure would.

Then he wanted her to watch him, to be completely vulnerable to her. He'd never wanted that with anyone, but he trusted this woman. She saw through all his bull-shit and baggage and wanted him anyway. And she didn't make him feel like she was doing him a favor by being with him.

She wanted him with a desperation he could see clearly in her eyes. They were both completely gone for each other and he was glad he wasn't alone in this all-con-suming hunger.

The tingling at the base of his spine built and crested, his balls pulled up tight as he felt his own orgasm coming up fast and hard. He wanted to slow down but there was no stopping it. Not this first time. Not after a year of lust-ing after her.

She dug her fingers into his back, her breathing out of control.

He reached between their bodies again, tweaked her clit. Her head fell back against the stairs, her mouth part-ing on a silent cry as she started clenching around him again, her inner walls milking him harder and harder.

When her back bowed tight and she cried out again, he let go of his control, thrusting hard inside her, taking everything she had to offer. He emptied himself inside her until he practically collapsed.

Instead of doing just that, he rolled to the side, half dragging her with him. The stairs were uncomfortable as shit, but he didn't care. Not when Ruby laid her head against his chest, sighed contentedly.

"That was…" She didn't finish, just let out another happy sigh as she slid her hand over his stomach.

"*Mi futura nuera* means my future daughter-in-law, by the way," he murmured after a few moments, his breathing returning to normal. He wondered if she remembered what his mom had said to her on Monday.

Ruby lifted her head, blinked at him once, her blue eyes wide. "Wh…I don't even know what to say to that."

"Don't say anything. I'm just telling you. And I'm also telling you she's probably right." He threw the 'probably' in in an attempt not to freak her out completely. Putting himself out there for her like this, especially when he'd just come to terms with the fact that she wanted him as much as he wanted her, made him feel vulnerable in a way he'd never experienced.

"God, I love you." Her voice was low as she leaned in, brushed her lips over his.

He jerked in surprise at the words, hadn't expected her to say them so soon, or at all. Something he hadn't realized had been missing filled his chest with happiness. "Ruby—"

"You don't have to say it back," she said simply. She was telling the truth. It was clear in her bright blue eyes.

He shook his head. "I do love you and I don't care if it's too soon. I know what I feel." Because he'd never felt anything like it. Not even close. It had to be love and he wasn't questioning it.

She gave him one of her brilliant smiles that lit up her whole face, and kissed him again.

He knew without a doubt that he was the luckiest guy in the world. And he was never letting her go.

CHAPTER EIGHTEEN

Ford slid his hand over Raegan's bare hip, squeezed once just to reassure himself she was okay. They'd been back at his place for hours and she'd long since crashed. He had a feeling she'd be sleeping a while. After such a scare it was only human nature to shut down, re-group. Sleep was sometimes the only way people could deal with shit. He knew that too well.

Unfortunately for him, sleep was elusive. Pushing out a sigh, he rolled onto his back. Part of him wanted to wake her up, but it would be selfish. He eased off the bed, headed into his bathroom. It was still dark out, but he wouldn't be going back to sleep anytime soon. Once the water was hot enough he stepped under the jets, let them pound against his back and shoulders.

It didn't do much to ease the tension as he relived eve-rything. He'd barely thought when he'd tackled that guy, had simply reacted using all of his training. He rubbed his hands over his face, slinging water off as he dropped them to his sides.

When he opened his eyes he found Raegan stepping into the shower with him. He blinked, surprised by how quiet she'd been. "You're awake?" His voice was still raspy from sleep.

She didn't respond, just stepped right up to him, wrapping her arms around him as the water cascaded over them.

He held her close, savoring the feel of her full breasts against his chest as he rubbed a hand down her spine. "Sorry if the shower woke you up."

"It didn't," she murmured against his chest. "I've been having weird dreams."

Probably nightmares. "That might happen for a while."

She shuddered in his arms and pulled her head back to look up at him. Wordlessly she reached between their bodies and grasped his already hardening cock. It was pretty much guaranteed he was turned on if Raegan was naked and in his arms.

"We don't have to do anything," he said quietly as she started stroking him, once, twice... He groaned.

The grin she gave him was pure, wicked Raegan. She liked to tease him, he'd learned. "I know. I want to," she said right before dropping to her knees.

After everything she'd been through he thought he should be the one comforting her, but holy fuck... His hips rolled at the feel of her lips wrapped around his cock.

She made little sounds of pleasure as she ran her tongue up the length of him. When he realized she was touching herself between her legs, he about lost it.

"You stroking that pussy, baby?" he rasped out. He wished he could see her hand moving, her fingers dipping inside herself.

She hummed against his cock, kept sucking him. He clenched his jaw, focused on not coming as she gripped the base of him, squeezed once. The sensual woman might not talk much during sex, but hell, she didn't need to.

He could talk enough for both of them. Especially when he knew it got her hot. "Does sucking me off get you wet?"

She moaned against him now, her strokes getting faster, the grip on the base of his cock just a little harder.

He wanted to let her keep going, to find release in her mouth, but he wanted inside her tight body even more. Though it pained him to do so, he pulled his hips back. She made a protesting sound until he lifted her up, pinned her against the tile wall.

Feeling frantic with the need to get inside her, he crushed his mouth to hers as he cupped her mound. Stroking a finger against her folds he found out exactly how slick she was for him. In that moment, words eluded him.

He just needed inside this woman. She'd completely stolen his heart and today he could have lost her. That knowledge pierced him deep, sliced up a part of him he didn't even know existed. What he'd thought was love before, what he'd had with his ex, was absolutely nothing compared to what he already felt for Raegan.

If he'd lost her... God, he couldn't even go there. Not if he wanted to remain sane.

Raegan gripped his shoulders and lifted herself up, wrapping her legs around him as he thrust inside her.

Groaning, he paused, buried fully inside her as he looked down at her. Her blue eyes were heavy lidded with a hunger that mirrored his own. There was so much he wanted to say to her, but he wasn't sure he could find the right words, and didn't want to ruin this moment anyway.

He wanted to ask her to move in with him starting tomorrow but it was too soon. Or he guessed it was. Hell if he knew. All he knew was that he wanted to wake up to her face always, wanted to see her face every night before he went to sleep.

She gave him a teasing smile, rolled her hips against his once, a clear signal that he better start moving.

Reaching between their bodies, he rubbed his thumb over her clit. Her eyes closed and her head fell back against the tile on a sigh as he began stroking her with just the right amount of pressure. He'd learned what she liked quickly and she was so open with her pleasure and what she needed from him.

When her breathing grew erratic and her fingers dug into his shoulders with just a bit more pressure he knew she was close.

So was he. The base of his spine tingled, his balls pulled up tight as he held back from coming. Not yet.

He began thrusting in steady, even strokes, keeping her pinned against the wall. "Come for me, Raegan," he murmured, desperate to see the pleasure on her face, to feel her climaxing around him.

Her eyes opened at his words, her chest rising and falling more erratically as he continued stroking her clit.

When he pinched it oh so lightly, she jerked against him, burying her face against his neck on a cry of ecstasy. He felt her teeth barely dig into his flesh as her inner walls clenched around his cock, milking him harder and harder.

As she cried out his name, he let go of his own control.

Gripping her ass, he pulled her away from the wall and thrust harder, driving into her over and over as his own orgasm overtook him. He loved that he got to come inside her with no barrier. He never wanted anything between them, literally or figuratively.

She was his and he was most definitely hers. The woman completely owned him.

As he came down from his climax, he leaned against the opposite wall with her still wrapped around him. Jets of water still pounded down against them, but all he could focus on was Raegan. She laid her head against his shoulder, laughed softly.

"Laughing while I'm still inside you?" He nipped her earlobe.

"Just thinking that you've turned me into a total freaking nympho."

"That's a bad thing?"

She laughed again. "No. Not at all. I'm also thinking that you're probably going to have to carry me back to the bedroom. I'm feeling pretty useless right now."

He could hear the drowsiness in her voice, feel the laxness in her muscles as she wrapped around him. Yeah, she'd be ready to go back to sleep soon. Which was good. He wanted her to get the rest her body needed.

"That's not a problem," he murmured. "But first..." Though he didn't want to put her down, he set her on the small built-in bench and grabbed a bottle of body wash and lathered soap between her legs.

She squirmed slightly, watching him carefully. "You're the sweetest man I've ever met."

Uncomfortable with the praise, he didn't say anything. Just rinsed her off before grabbing towels for the two of them. He was surprised she let him dry her off and carry her back to bed, but he found he liked taking care of her like this.

When he tucked her back against his chest and held her close, he knew that he could get used to this. For once, he wasn't afraid of the future, wasn't worried that things would go south with the two of them.

He knew what type of woman Raegan was and he was damn lucky to have found her. Now that he had, he wasn't letting her go.

Three months later

"Honey, I'm home," Raegan called out, making Ford laugh from the kitchen.

"I'm slaving away over a hot stove." He turned at the sound of her shoes clicking across the tile floor.

"So, I'm guessing you ordered takeout?" She hung her purse on one of the wall hooks and slipped her heeled boots off, leaving them haphazardly where they fell. Which he'd learned was standard Raegan. It was a miracle she remembered to hang her purse up. Normally in the mornings she ran around looking for her purse and keys because she couldn't remember where she'd left them.

He just grinned, drinking in the sight of her. In bare feet and a dark blue sweater dress with a loose belt, she looked good enough to eat. He couldn't wait to strip her naked later. "You'll just have to come out on the patio and see."

"That sounds like heaven," she sighed.

Since the weather had started to slowly shift into fall it was cool enough to eat outside, so they'd been having dinner by the pool over the last week.

"Long day?" he asked.

She nodded, moving into him for a hug. She settled her face against his chest, just held him. "Yeah. Good, but long. We got a new client today and she's exhausting. Athena wants me to handle this job totally by myself."

"You'll do great."

"Yeah, maybe. It's still a little scary."

After everything she'd been through, he figured this would be a piece of cake for her. But he didn't say that. He'd come to learn that she simply liked to worry about work stuff, but always came through, always did a fantastic job above and beyond what was expected.

"I already know the answer, but how was your day?" she asked, pulling back.

He smiled down at her, amazed that this woman was in his life. He hoped to make it a permanent thing and was terrified he'd screw up tonight. "Awesome. The SF guys who did the training class really knew their stuff. And...we got to shoot a lot of weapons. The new guys were in heaven."

She just snorted. "That's why I knew you had an awesome day."

"Come on. Let's head out to the pool. Maybe we can swim after dinner?"

She lightly pinched his side as she stepped back. "I know that look and I'm not swimming naked."

He stifled a laugh. "My eighty-year-old and seventy-year-old neighbors aren't spying on us."

"You never know and I'm not taking the chance."

"I seriously love you," he murmured, kissing the top of her head.

"Well you're gonna love me more when you find out what I got for your birthday."

"What?"

"Nope. You don't get it until next month. I just wanted to torture you a little."

"I never realized you have a little mean streak."

She just grinned as he opened the back door. "Don't you forget it." She paused three steps outside, staring out at the transformed patio.

He'd had a little help with the idea—okay, a lot of help—but he'd set everything up himself. He'd moved all the patio furniture under the overhang into the garage and replaced it with a bunch of multicolored blankets and pillows. He'd hung up twinkle lights across the entire lanai and placed flameless candles in the shape of a big heart around the blankets. There were even different colored floating LED lights in the pool. He'd wanted to completely change the atmosphere so it was romantic but private.

Because he knew Raegan would have hated a public proposal. Hell, he just hoped she said yes.

It was pretty early in their relationship, but he'd given her a key to his place a week after the shooting, they'd said they loved each other two weeks after and she pretty much lived here now. She already took up half of his closet and he wanted her living with him permanently.

Raegan was it for him. He couldn't imagine a world without her in it. Didn't want to.

When she turned back to him, eyes wide, he was already on one knee, the box open. His hands actually shook as he held it out to her. "Marry me?"

She nodded, tears glittering in her eyes as she held her left hand out and cupped his cheek with her right. "Yes."

He loved how affectionate she was, how she never held anything back. Not her emotions, nothing. With Raegan, what you saw was what you got.

He slid the diamond on her finger, felt a weight lifting he hadn't realized he was carrying when he saw it glittering under the moonlight and twinkle lights. Hell yeah, she was his and he wanted the whole damn world to know she was taken.

Standing, he pulled her into his arms, brushed his mouth over hers lightly before deepening the kiss. Somehow he pulled back. "I got your favorite champagne." He motioned to the ice bucket in the middle of the blankets.

Smiling brightly, she practically dragged him to the bed of blankets. "If you do have pervert neighbors, they're about to get a show," she whispered, already making quick work of his belt buckle.

Laughing, he pinned her underneath him and captured her mouth again. He couldn't wait to spend the rest of his life with her. Raegan was the best thing that had ever happened to him and he planned to show her every day just how much she meant to him.

Thank you for reading Secret Obsession. I really hope you enjoyed it and that you'll consider leaving a review at one of your favorite online retailers.

If you would like to read more, turn the page for a sneak peek of more of my work. And if you don't want to miss any future releases, please feel free to join my newsletter. I only send out a newsletter for new releases or sales news. Find the signup link on my website: http://www.katiereus.com

ACKNOWLEDGMENTS

As always I owe thanks to Kari Walker! I couldn't ask for a better critique partner or best friend. Thank you to Julia Ganis for taking on this project. Working with you was a wonderful experience. Many thanks to Jaycee with Sweet 'N Spicy Designs for another beautiful cover. To Tammy, Grace, and Joanna, thank you for your help confirming a translation. For my readers, you keep asking for more Red Stone books and I'm thrilled to bring you another one. Thank you all for reading this series and your wonderfully supportive emails. For my husband and son, you guys are my rocks. I'm also very grateful to Sarah for all the behind-the-scenes stuff that she does. Thanks to her, I get to write more! Last but never least, I'm grateful to God.

COMPLETE BOOKLIST

Red Stone Security Series
No One to Trust
Danger Next Door
Fatal Deception
Miami, Mistletoe & Murder
His to Protect
Breaking Her Rules
Protecting His Witness
Sinful Seduction
Under His Protection
Deadly Fallout
Sworn to Protect
Secret Obsession
Love Thy Enemy

The Serafina: Sin City Series
First Surrender
Sensual Surrender
Sweetest Surrender
Dangerous Surrender

Deadly Ops Series
Targeted
Bound to Danger
Chasing Danger (novella)
Shattered Duty
Edge of Danger
A Covert Affair

Non-series Romantic Suspense
Running From the Past
Dangerous Secrets
Killer Secrets
Deadly Obsession
Danger in Paradise
His Secret Past
Retribution
Merry Christmas, Baby

Paranormal Romance
Destined Mate
Protector's Mate
A Jaguar's Kiss
Tempting the Jaguar
Enemy Mine
Heart of the Jaguar

Moon Shifter Series
Alpha Instinct
Lover's Instinct (novella)
Primal Possession
Mating Instinct
His Untamed Desire (novella)
Avenger's Heat
Hunter Reborn
Protective Instinct (novella)

Darkness Series
Darkness Awakened
Taste of Darkness
Beyond the Darkness
Hunted by Darkness
Into the Darkness

ABOUT THE AUTHOR

Katie Reus is the *New York Times* and *USA Today* bestselling author of the Red Stone Security series, the Moon Shifter series and the Deadly Ops series. She fell in love with romance at a young age thanks to books she pilfered from her mom's stash. Years later she loves reading romance almost as much as she loves writing it.

However, she didn't always know she wanted to be a writer. After changing majors many times, she finally graduated summa cum laude with a degree in psychology. Not long after that she discovered a new love. Writing. She now spends her days writing dark paranormal romance and sexy romantic suspense.

For more information on Katie please visit her website: www.katiereus.com. Also find her on twitter @katiereus or visit her on facebook at: www.facebook.com/katiereusauthor.

Made in the USA
Middletown, DE
30 September 2016